基礎文法寶典 ②
Essential English Usage & Grammar

編著／J. B. Alter

審訂／劉美皇　呂香瑩

三民書局

Grammar Guru

國家圖書館出版品預行編目資料

Essential English Usage & Grammar 基礎文法寶典
／J. B. Alter編著;劉美皇,呂香瑩審訂.－－初版
一刷.－－臺北市：三民，2008
　冊；　公分

　ISBN 978-957-14-5102-2　（平裝）

　1.英語 2.語法

805.16　　　　　　　　　　　　　　　97018552

© Essential English Usage & Grammar
基礎文法寶典 2

編 著 者	J. B. Alter
審　　訂	劉美皇　呂香瑩
企劃編輯	王伊平
責任編輯	彭彥哲
美術設計	郭雅萍
發 行 人	劉振強
著作財產權人	三民書局股份有限公司
發 行 所	三民書局股份有限公司
	地址　臺北市復興北路386號
	電話　(02)25006600
	郵撥帳號　0009998-5
門 市 部	(復北店)臺北市復興北路386號
	(重南店)臺北市重慶南路一段61號
出版日期	初版一刷　2008年11月
編　　號	S 807510

行政院新聞局登記證局版臺業字第○二○○號

有著作權・不准侵害

ISBN　978-957-14-5102-2　（平裝）

http://www.sanmin.com.tw　三民網路書店

序

如果說，單字是英文的血肉，文法就是英文的骨架。想要打好英文基礎，兩者實應相輔相成，缺一不可。

只是，單字可以死背，文法卻不然。

學習文法，如果沒有良師諄諄善誘，沒有好書細細剖析，只落得個見樹不見林，徒然勞心費力，實在可惜。

Guru 原義指的是精通於某領域的「達人」，因此，這一套「文法 Guru」系列叢書，本著 Guru「導師」的精神，要告訴您：親愛的，我把英文文法變簡單了！

「文法 Guru」系列，適用對象廣泛，從初習英文的超級新鮮人、被文法糾纏得寢食難安的中學生，到鎮日把玩英文的專業行家，都能在這一套系列叢書中找到最適合自己的夥伴。

深願「文法 Guru」系列，能成為您最好的學習夥伴，伴您一同輕鬆悠遊英文學習的美妙世界。

有了「文法 Guru」，文法輕鬆上路！

前言

「**基礎文法寶典**」一套五冊，是專為中學生與一般社會大眾所設計，作為基礎課程教材或是課外自學之用。

英語教師往往對結構、句型、語法等為主的教學模式再熟悉不過。然而，現在學界普遍意識到**文法在語言學習的過程中亦佔有一席之地**，少了文法這一環，英語教學便顯得空洞。有鑑於此，市場上漸漸興起一股「**功能性文法**」的風潮。功能性文法旨在列舉用法並協助讀者熟悉文法專有名詞，而後者便是用以解釋及界定一語言各種功能的利器。

本套書各冊內容編排詳盡，涵蓋所有用法及文法要點；除此之外，本套書最強調的便是從不斷的練習中學好英文。每章所附的練習題皆經特別設計，提供讀者豐富多元的演練題型，舉凡**完成** (completion)、**修正** (modification)、**轉換** (conversion)、**合併** (integration)、**重述** (restatement)、**改寫** (alteration)、**變形** (transformation) 及**代換** (transposition)，應有盡有。

熟讀此書，將可幫助您完全理解各種文法及正確的表達方式，讓您在課業學習或日常生活上的英文程度突飛猛進。

給讀者的話

本書一套共五本，共分為二十一章，從最基礎的各式詞類介紹，一直到動詞的進階應用、基本書寫概念等，涵蓋所有的基本文法要義，為您建立一個完整的自修體系，並以豐富多樣的練習題為最大特色。

本書的主要細部單元包括：

USAGE PRACTICE →每個文法條目說明之下，皆有大量的例句或用法實例，讓您充分了解該文法規則之實際應用方式。

注意→很多文法規則皆有特殊的應用，或者是因應不同情境而產生相關變化，這些我們都以較小字的提示，列在本單元中。

但是我們會用→文法規則的例外情況也不少，我們在這單元直接以舉例的方式，說明這些不依循規則的情況。

小練習→每節介紹後，會有針對該節內容所設計的一段習題，可讓您即時驗證前面所學的內容。

應用練習→每章的內容結束後，我們都提供了非常充分的應用練習，而且題型豐富，各有其學習功能。建議您不要急於在短時間內將練習做完，而是漸進式地逐步完成，這樣可達成更好的學習效果。

本書文法內容完善，習題亦兼具廣度與深度，是您自修學習之最佳選擇，也可作為文法疑難的查閱參考，值得您細細研讀，慢慢體會。

基礎文法寶典 ❷
Essential English Usage & Grammar

目次

基礎文法寶典❷
Essential English Usage & Grammar

Chapter 6 介系詞

6-1 介系詞的用法

> 介系詞常用來表示名詞或代名詞與句子其餘部份的關係，同時也可以用來表示位置、時間或運動的方向。

(a) 介系詞常和某些字詞連用。

USAGE PRACTICE

▶ I bought this jar **at** the market. 我在市場買了這個罐子。

▶ She is good **at** cooking. 她擅長烹飪。

▶ She was hiding the camera **from** her brother. 她把相機藏起來不讓她弟弟發現。

(b) 介系詞原本應該要放在受詞之前，但如果受詞是疑問詞（即 wh- 問句），疑問詞會移到句首，介系詞則通常留在後面。

USAGE PRACTICE

▶ What are you looking **for**? 你在找什麼？

▶ Who is she smiling **at**? 她在對誰微笑？

▶ Who is this book written **by**? 這本書是誰寫的？

(c) 用不定詞片語當補語修飾前面的名詞時，介系詞也會出現在受詞之後。

USAGE PRACTICE

▶ These are good things to talk **about**. 這些是值得一提的好事。

▶ The water is not hot enough to boil the noodles **in**. 這水還沒有熱到可以煮麵。

▶ He has no one to talk **to**. 他沒有講話的對象。

(d) 在限定用法的關係子句中，先行詞若是受詞，介系詞常放在子句的最後面，而且關係代名詞可以省略。

USAGE PRACTICE

► This is the vase (that) I was telling you **about**.

這就是我過去一直跟你講的那個花瓶。

► The painting (that) he is pointing **at** costs two hundred dollars.

他正指的那一幅畫價值兩佰元。

► We are talking about the house (that) we used to live **in**.

我們正在談論我們過去住的那間房子。

小練習

請在空格中填入合適的介系詞。

1. Which drawer did he put his clothes _____ ?

2. He is not a difficult man to work _____ .

3. Is this the house you read _____ in the newspaper?

4. She does not have enough money to live _____ for the rest of the month.

5. Where did you think the voices came _____ ?

6. This is the man I was speaking _____ .

7. Where is the knife I usually sharpen my pencils _____ ?

8. I wonder what she is dressing up _____ ?

9. We don't know what he is hinting _____ .

10. Who is he angry _____ ? Is he complaining _____ her again?

11. What are those papers you were looking _____ just now?

12. Those players are too expert for you to compete _____ .

13. Who is she waiting _____ ? Could it be that person I saw her _____ last night?

14. These are the keys the child was playing _____ yesterday.

15. I know the girl you were walking _____ just now. She is the girl whose essays the teacher was very pleased _____ .

16. You can use this kettle to boil the water _____ . Are you going to make tea _____ yourself?

☞ 更多相關習題請見本章應用練習 Part 1～Part 3。

6-2 動詞 + 介系詞

ABOUT

complain **about** 抱怨	bring **about** 引起	consult **about** 商量
see **about** 處理	quarrel **about** 爭吵	talk **about** 談論
worry **about** 擔心	set **about** 攻擊	debate **about** 討論
joke **about** 開玩笑	think **about** 考慮	write **about** 寫關於…
dream **about** 夢見	care **about** 在乎	boast **about** 誇耀
walk **about** 到處走	hang **about** 徘徊閒逛	lay **about** 猛烈攻擊

▶ The new manager has brought **about** some changes. 這個新經理已經引起了一些改變。

▶ He hung **about** the street waiting for her to come out. 他在街上徘徊閒逛，等她出來。

▶ If he goes **about** behaving like this, he will get thrown out.
  如果他開始像這樣的行為，他會被人攆走。

ACROSS

come **across** 偶遇	walk **across** 走過	put **across** 使被理解

AFTER

run **after** 追求	look **after** 照顧	take **after** 與…相似

▶ Mark takes **after** his father in a love for the outdoor life.
  馬克在喜愛戶外生活方面像他的父親。

▶ Since he was beaten in the game, he has been thirsting **after** revenge.
  自從他之前在比賽中被擊敗，他就一直渴望雪恥。

▶ They inquired **after** my health. 他們問候我的健康狀況。

AGAINST

compete **against** 與…競爭	bump **against** 撞到	fight **against** 與…搏鬥
brush **against** 擦到	turn **against** 敵視，反對	appeal **against** 上訴
secure...**against** 避免遭受	guard **against** 預防	clash **against** 撞上
unite **against** 聯合對抗	battle **against** 與…作戰	tell **against** 對…有不利影響

AMONG

divide...**among** 在…之間分發

AROUND

look **around** 環顧四周　　travel **around** 到處旅行　　get **around** 散播（消息）

hang **round** 閒蕩

ASIDE

set **aside** 不顧，不理會

AT

aim **at** 瞄準	peep **at** 偷看	arrive **at** 到達
stare **at** 凝視	guess **at** 猜測	excel **at** 擅於
glance **at** 瞥見	get **at** 嘲笑	laugh **at** 嘲笑
jump **at** 急切地接受	sniff **at** 輕視	point **at** 指著
look **at** 注視	throw **at** 對…丟	play **at** 假扮
stick **at** 堅持		

▶ They are always getting **at** me for being the teacher's pet. 他們總嘲笑我是老師的寵兒。

▶ I jumped **at** the chance for a voyage. 我迫不及待地接受這個航海旅行的機會。

AWAY

take **away** 拿走	get **away** 離開	carry **away** 帶走
give **away** 洩露	throw **away** 扔掉	

BACK

keep...**back** 隱瞞

BEHIND

stand **behind** 站在後面　　leave...**behind** 忘了帶

BESIDE

stand **beside** 站在…的旁邊

BETWEEN

lie **between** 位於（兩者）之間　　share **between** 在（兩者）之間分配…

BY

stand **by** 旁觀	stop **by** 順道拜訪	pass **by** 經過
come **by** 得到	drop **by** 順道拜訪	put **by** 儲存

stand **by** 準備，待命　　　　go **by** 憑…判斷

▶ She put **by** some money for the children's fees. 她存了一些錢當小孩的學費用。

▶ They stood **by** in case of an emergency. 他們待命以防意外。

▶ I'll drop/stop/call **by** to see you on my way back. 我回來的時候會順道拜訪你。

▶ How did he come **by** such a beautiful painting? 他是怎麼得到這樣一幅美麗的畫？

▶ He swears **by** aspirins as a cure for the flu. 他非常相信阿斯匹林可以治療流行性感冒。

▶ A real friend sticks **by** you when you are in trouble.

　當你處於困境時，真正的朋友還是支持你。

DOWN

break **down** 弄壞，毀壞	cast **down** 使沮喪	cut **down** 減少
nail/pin **down** 確定	play **down** 貶低	run **down** 詆毀；撞倒
shake **down** 徹底搜查	take **down** 記下	turn **down** 拒絕
shout **down** 大叫使（某人的聲音）聽不到		burn **down** 燒毀
write **down** 寫下	put **down** 放下	knock **down** 降低
lay **down** 將…放下	pull **down** 拆毀	set **down** 記下

▶ He turned **down** my offer since he had a better one from somebody else.

　他拒絕我的提議，因為別人給他一個更好的。

▶ The enemy laid **down** their arms after the battle. 交戰後，敵軍放下他們的武器。

▶ These men are willing to lay **down** their lives for their country. 這些人願意為國犧牲生命。

▶ The old man was run **down** while crossing the street. 這個老人在過街時被汽車撞倒。

FOR

beg **for** 懇求	petition **for** 請求	mistake **for** 把…誤認為
hunt **for** 搜尋	bargain **for** 預料	wish **for** 期望
reach **for** 伸出手拿…	wait **for** 等待	blame **for** 因…責備
volunteer **for** 志願做…	prepare **for** 為…準備	ask **for** 要求
account **for** 解釋	angle **for** 謀取	answer **for** 對…負責
call **for** 需要	pass **for** 被認為	stand **for** 代表
sail **for** 航向…	take...**for** 將…視為	work **for** 為…工作
look **for** 尋找	mourn **for** 悼念	long **for** 渴望

search **for** 尋找　　　　　　　　apologize **for** 為…道歉

▶ When I saw Peter just now, I took him **for** Paul. 我剛才看見彼得時，誤以為他是保羅。

FORTH

set **forth** 闡釋

FORWARD

put **forward** 提出

FROM

dismiss **from** 摒除	divert...**from** 從…轉移	inherit **from** 繼承
divorce...**from** 使分開	abstain **from** 戒除	free...**from** 解放
disconnect...**from** 分離	shrink **from** 退避	buy...**from** 向…買
escape **from** 脫離	abstract...**from** 從…抽出來	prevent...**from** 阻止
hide **from** 隱藏	refrain **from** 忍住	exclude...**from** 把…排除在外
escape **from** 從…逃走	come **from** 來自	release...**from** 免除
graduate **from** 畢業於	disappear **from** 自…消失不見	

IN

confide **in** 向…吐露秘密	sink **in** 被理解	meddle **in** 干涉
give **in** 讓步、屈服	confirm **in** 堅信	include **in** 包括
involve **in** 牽涉	turn **in** 歸還	increase **in**（在…方面）增加
dabble **in** 涉獵	join **in** 參加	fill **in** 填入
interfere **in** 干涉	fail **in** 未盡到（義務等）	invest **in** 投資
indulge **in** 沉迷於	bring **in** 產生	break **in** 闖入
swim **in** 浸，泡	take **in** 欺騙；理解	call **in** 請求收回
drop **in** 突然拜訪		

INTO

pry **into** 探聽	walk **into** 不慎陷入	fall **into** 陷入
dive **into** 埋首於	run **into** 偶遇	dip **into** 稍加探究
flow **into** 流入	inject...**into** 把…注入	break **into** 闖入
go **into** 調查	let...**into** 讓…進入	talk...**into** 勸說

crash **into** 撞上	pour **into** 注入	read...**into** 認為⋯意味著
cut **into** 插嘴	put **into**（船）駛進	bump **into** 偶遇
make...**into** 把⋯做成	look **into** 調查	expand **into** 發展成⋯

OF

think **of** 想到	assure **of** 保證	complain **of** 抱怨
dispose **of** 處理	approve **of** 贊成	consist **of** 由⋯組成
tell **of** 講述	beware **of** 小心	speak **of** 提及
clear...**of** 使⋯乾淨	brag **of** 吹牛	

▶ What is to become **of** you when this house is sold? 房子賣掉後，你會怎麼樣呢？

OFF

break **off** 中斷	leave **off** 停止	round **off** 圓滿結束
pack **off** 把某人打發走	throw **off** 扔掉	work **off** 發洩
palm **off** 欺騙某人	see...**off** 為⋯送行	set **off** 引發
show **off** 炫耀	write **off** 取消	switch **off** 關掉
turn **off** 關掉	carry **off** 贏得（獎項）	let **off** 寬恕
pass **off** 冒充；（活動）進行	get **off** 逃脫處罰	come **off** 脫離；離開
polish **off** 趕快做完	give **off** 發出	put **off** 延遲；使不喜歡
tip **off** 向⋯透露消息	touch **off** 引發	take **off** 把⋯拿開；休假
strike **off** 刪除	tell **off** 斥責	

▶ The football match was put **off** because of the heavy rain. 因為大雨，橄欖球賽延期。

▶ I saw him **off** at the airport. 我在機場為他送行。

▶ We managed to keep **off** the wild beasts with torches. 我們設法用火把防止野獸接近。

▶ I am taking a few days **off** at the end of the month. 我要在這個月底休假幾天。

▶ They may let you **off** if you apologize. 如果你道歉，他們可能會饒恕你。

▶ I was cut **off** in the middle of my telephone conversation. 我電話講到一半時就被切斷了。

▶ The smell of rotting fish put me **off** my food. 腐壞的魚的惡臭使我不想吃東西。

▶ The spy passed himself **off** as a workman and entered the building.

　 這個間諜冒充工人，進入這棟建築物。

▶ They pulled **off** the most daring robbery of our time.

他們完成了我們這個時期最大膽的搶案。

▶ I was told **off** for behaving so rudely. 我因為行事粗魯而被責罵。

▶ The meeting was called **off** at the last minute. 這會議在最後一刻被取消了。

▶ The police gave chase, but he managed to shake them **off**.
警方追捕，但他設法擺脫了他們。

▶ That minor incident touched **off** a terrible war. 那小小的事情件引發了一場可怕的戰爭。

ON

agree **on** 同意	step **on** 踩	experiment **on** 實驗
keep **on** 繼續	confer **on** 商議	spy **on** 暗中監視
lie **on** 依據	harp **on** 反覆述說	elaborate **on** 詳細講述
depend **on** 依靠	lecture **on** 講課	focus **on** 集中於
bank **on** 指望	bring **on** 引起	call **on** 拜訪
rely **on** 依賴	carry **on** 繼續	figure **on** 料想
get **on** 進展	tell **on** 影響	jump **on** 責罵
light **on** 無意瞥見	look **on** 看待，考慮	live **on** 靠…生活
play **on** 演奏	put **on** 穿上	round **on** 突然攻擊
carry **on** 繼續	sit **on** 擱置	sleep **on** 留待次日再考慮
take **on** 雇用	switch **on** 打開（開關）	trade **on** 利用
turn **on** 打開；突然襲擊	work **on** 影響	spill **on** 溢出，灑落
inflict **on** 給予（打擊等）	sponge **on** 依賴他人為生	

▶ Did you call **on** Jane when you went to Port Haven? 你去哈文港時，你拜訪珍了嗎？

▶ We are counting **on** your help at the concert. 我們指望你在演奏會時幫忙。

OUT

back **out** 取消	bear **out** 證實	call **out** 大聲叫出
bring **out** 拿出	carry **out** 實行；執行	lay **out** 用（錢）
make **out** 理解	put **out** 拔出	pass **out** 昏倒
pick **out** 挑選	play **out** 結束	spin **out** 拉長
rule **out** 排除	see **out** 持續到結束	speak **out** 大聲說
look **out** 挑選	cut **out** 刪去	hold **out** 給予，提供

iron **out** 消除，解決	kick **out** 解雇	knock **out** 擊倒
stick...**out** 伸出	point **out** 指出	take **out** 除去
throw **out** 扔掉	turn **out** 關掉；生產	leave **out** 省略
walk...**out** 把…帶出去	wash...**out** 把…洗掉	wipe **out** 消滅
find **out** 找出	work **out** 解決；想出	

▶ They worked **out** that they would have exactly two dollars left after shopping.
他們算出在採買之後他們會剛好剩下兩元。

▶ This factory turns **out** electrical appliances. 這家工廠生產電器。

▶ He will bear me **out** on what I have to say. 他會支持我必須講的話。

▶ They carried **out** his orders to the letter. 他們精確地執行他的命令。

▶ I can't make **out** anything from her letter. 我完全看不懂她的信。

OVER

fly **over** 飛越	jump **over** 躍過	talk **over** 商談
give **over** 停止	take **over** 接收	bowl **over** 撞倒；使驚訝
chew **over** 仔細考慮	hold **over** 延期	run **over** 快速閱讀
stand **over** 監督	see **over** 參觀	tick **over** 緩慢進行
win **over** 說服	tide...**over** 幫助…度過難關	

▶ She watched **over** the baby as it slept. 嬰兒睡覺時，她看顧它。

▶ A change suddenly came **over** her. 她突然感到有變化了。

▶ The general took **over** command yesterday. 這將軍昨天接收了指揮權。

PAST

| march **past** 大步走過 | walk **past** 走過 |

THROUGH

go **through** 檢查	pass **through** 經歷；通過	pull **through** 渡過危機
skim **through** 略讀	put **through** 完成	run **through** 耗盡
see **through** 看穿	get **through** 通過	

TO

| address **to** 對…說 | belong **to** 屬於 | confess **to** 承認 |

confine **to** 把…限制在	adjust **to** 適應	connect **to** 連接
object **to** 反對	reply **to** 回覆	amount **to** 總計
consent **to** 同意	pretend **to** 自稱	agree **to** 同意
listen **to** 傾聽	look **to** 倚賴	come **to** 甦醒過來；共計
run **to** 擴展到	see **to** 處理	set **to** 開始
stick **to** 堅持	take **to** 喜歡	go **to** 前往
succumb **to** 屈服於	promise...**to** 答應把…給…	

▶ It is your duty as a host to <u>see</u> **to** your guests. 照顧你的客人是你做主人的責任。

▶ Remember me **to** Raymond when you see him. 當你見到雷蒙時，代我問候他。

UNDER

knuckle **under** 屈服

UP

back **up** 支持	bear **up** 挺住	call **up** 回憶；打電話
lay **up**（因病）臥床不起	cut **up** 切碎	give **up** 放棄
hang **up** 掛電話	size **up** 估計	hold **up** 搶劫；使耽擱
keep **up** 保持	lap **up** 舔食	shut **up** 閉嘴
line **up** 使排成行	make **up** 編造	warm **up** 加熱；使活耀
polish **up** 改善	show **up** 出現	take **up** 對…感興趣
shake **up** 振作，激勵	snap **up** 搶購	throw **up** 嘔吐
touch **up** 修改，潤色	work **up** 激發，使激動	wind **up** 使結束
wake **up** 使醒來	stand...**up** 失約	step **up** 增加，加快
put **up** 搭（帳篷）	turn **up** 翻起	pick **up** 拾起；獲得（消息）
think **up** 想出	climb **up** 爬上	lock **up** 將…上鎖
save **up** 儲存	set **up** 建立	cover **up** 掩蓋
kick **up** 激起	pull **up** 向上拉	run **up** 積欠
reckon **up** 計算	rub **up** 擦亮	

▶ He <u>gave</u> **up** studying when his father died. 當他父親過世時，他放棄了學業。

▶ The traffic jam <u>held</u> us **up** for three hours. 交通阻塞使我們耽擱了三個小時。

▶ She <u>brought</u> them **up** in the right way. 她順利地把他們撫養長大。

▶ I am sure he made **up** that story. 我確信他捏造了那個故事。

▶ The program they drew **up** was not satisfactory. 他們所擬定的計畫並不令人滿意。

▶ They set **up** a committee to study the case. 他們成立一個委員會來研究這個案件。

▶ I rang him **up** and told him the news. 我打電話給他，告訴他這個消息。

▶ He took **up** gardening when he retired from his job. 退休後，他開始喜歡上園藝。

▶ I'll pick you **up** on the way. 我將會在途中去載你。

▶ He plucked **up** enough courage to knock on the door. 他鼓起足夠的勇氣去敲門。

▶ You should brush **up** your French before going to France. 去法國之前，你應該溫習法文。

▶ Mrs. Wilson ran **up** a huge bill at the dressmaker's and now she can't pay it.

威爾遜太太在裁縫店積欠了一大筆帳，現在她無法償還。

▶ I'll look him **up** when I'm in town. 當我在城裡的時候，我會去拜訪他。

▶ She picked **up** the information in Peggy's house. 她在佩姬家得知這個消息。

UPON
touch **upon** 涉及，提到

WITH		
acquaint **with** 使認識	cover...**with** 用…遮蓋	combine...**with** 使聯合
balance **with** 與…協調	equip...**with** 裝備	occupy...**with** 忙於
illustrate...**with** 用…來說明	meet **with** 與…會面	pair...**with** 與…配對
sit **with** 和…一起坐著	walk **with** 和…一起走路	talk **with** 和…講話
argue **with** 和…爭吵	bear **with** 忍受	toy **with** 玩弄；不認真考慮
collide **with** 與…衝撞	rhyme **with** 與…押韻	deal **with** 處理

WITHOUT	
go **without** 沒有…也可以	live **without** 沒有…而生存

6-3 名詞＋介系詞

ABOUT	
story **about** 關於…的故事	inquiry **about** 關於…的打聽
feeling **about** 對…的感覺	detail **about** 有關…的細節

discussion **about** 關於⋯的討論	excitement **about** 對⋯感到興奮

AGAINST

proof **against** 不利⋯的證據	grudge **against** 對⋯的怨恨
judgment **against** 不利⋯的判決	race **against** 與⋯的競賽
crime **against** 違反⋯的罪行	evidence **against** 不利⋯的證據
charge **against** 對⋯的指控	protest **against** 對⋯的抗議

AFTER

thirst **after** 對⋯的渴望

AMONG

quarrel **among**（三者以上）⋯之間的爭吵

AT

arrival **at** 到達	attendance **at** 出席
delight **at** 因⋯而高興	

BETWEEN

choice **between** 在（兩者）⋯間的抉擇	marriage **between** 某人和某人之間的婚姻
difference **between**（兩者）⋯間的差異	equality **between**（兩者）⋯間的平等
link **between**（兩者）⋯間的連結	compromise **between**（兩者）⋯間的妥協

BY

book **by** ⋯寫的書	portrait **by** ⋯畫的肖像

FOR

candidate **for** ⋯的候選人	need **for** 需要
witness **for** ⋯的目擊者	punishment **for** ⋯的處罰
reason **for** ⋯的原因	sympathy **for** 對⋯的同情
dislike **for** 憎惡	respect **for** 尊敬
warrant **for** ⋯的理由	taste **for** 愛好
reward **for** 做為⋯的報酬	substitute **for** ⋯的代替者
concern **for** 對⋯的關心	desire **for** 對⋯的渴望

appetite **for** 對…的愛好	fondness **for** 對…的喜好
ticket **for** …的票	evidence **for** 有利於…的證據
genius **for** 有…的才能	formula **for** …的配方
remedy **for** …的補救方法	

FROM

divorce **from** 與…離婚	alien **from** 來自…的外國人
refugee **from** 來自…的難民	departure **from** 從…離開
permission **from** …的同意	reply **from** …的回覆
answer **from** …的答覆	

IN

faith **in** 對…的信賴	graduate **in** 主修…的大學畢業生
progress **in** 在…的進步	confidence **in** 對…的信心
interest **in** 對…的興趣	improvement **in** 在…的改進
belief **in** 相信	origin **in** 起源於
delight **in** 以…為樂	specialist **in** …的專家
lesson **in** …的課程	experience **in** 在…的經驗
error **in** …的錯誤	superiority **in** 在…的優勢
expert **in** …的專家	

INTO

entry **into** …的入口	insight **into** 洞察
intrusion **into** 侵入	

OF

combination **of** …的結合	relative **of** …的親戚
exhibition **of** …的展示	description **of** …的描寫
result **of** …的結果	descendant **of** …的子孫
exchange **of** …的交換	proof **of** …的證明
collection **of** …的收集	ignorance **of** …的無知
end **of** …的結局	envy **of** …的羨慕對象

danger of …的危險	approval of …的同意
acceptance of …的接受	abundance of 大量的
group of 一群	a couple of 幾個;兩個
disregard of 忽視	dread of 懼怕
impression of 對…的印象	satisfaction of …的滿意
judge of …的裁判	example of …的例子

ON

emphasis on 強調	duty on 對…所課的稅
discussion on 有關…的討論	speech on 關於…的演講
shame on 羞辱	agreement on 有關…的協定
focus on 重點放在…	advice on 對…的建議
accent on （發音）強調,著重	influence on 對…的影響
outlook on 對…的看法	

OVER

control over 對…的控制	influence over 對…的影響
power over 對…有影響力	quarrel over 針對…爭吵
disagreement over 不同意	

▶ He has an advantage over us since he is older. 他比我們佔優勢,因為他年紀比較大。

TO

allusion to 提及	aversion to 對…的厭惡感
disgrace to …的恥辱	attitude to 對…的態度
alternative to …的替代	exposure to 暴露於…
access to 使用、接近…的權利	heir to 繼承…的人
danger to 對…是威脅	limit to 對…的限制
exception to …的例外	attention to 對…的注意
invitation to 參加…的邀約	

TOWARD

feeling toward 對…的感覺	disgust toward 對…的厭惡

affection **toward** 對…的愛	friendliness **toward** 對…的友好
behavior **toward** 對…的行為	indifference **toward** 對…的冷漠

UPON	
dependence **upon** 依賴…	impact **upon** 對…的影響

WITH	
familiarity **with** 通曉	competition **with** 與…的競賽
encounter **with** 與…的偶遇	feud **with** 與…的仇恨
fight **with** 和…的戰鬥	business **with** 和…的生意往來
struggle **with** 與…的拼鬥	war **with** 與…的戰爭
trouble **with** 有…的困難	battle **with** 與…的戰鬥
agreement **with** 同意	

6-4 形容詞 + 介系詞

ABOUT	
nervous **about** 擔心	upset **about** 對…感到心煩意亂
clear **about** 對…很確定	careful **about** 對…小心
worried **about** 為…感到擔憂	confused **about** 對…感到困惑
glad **about** 對…感到高興	anxious **about** 為…感到焦慮
annoyed **about** 對…感到氣惱	

▶ He was angry **about** the delay of the mail. 他對於郵件的耽擱感到生氣。

▶ His mother was anxious **about** his safety. 他的母親擔心他的安全。

▶ Are you certain **about** going on the excursion? 你確定會去遠足嗎？

▶ They are happy **about** being chosen for the team. 他們很高興被選為隊員。

▶ He is sorry **about** losing the money. 他為錢丟了而感到難過。

▶ What is he looking so pleased **about**? 什麼使他看起來如此高興？

▶ I am worried **about** my brother. 我擔心我弟弟。

AT	
annoyed **at** 對…感到生氣	surprised **at** 對…感到驚訝

pleased **at** 對…感到高興

amazed **at** 對…感到驚訝

shocked **at** 對…感到震驚

good **at** 擅於

marvelous **at** 對…感到驚奇

disappointed **at** 對…感到失望

poor **at** 不擅於

angry **at** 對…感到生氣

terrible **at** 不擅於

▶ I was <u>alarmed</u> **at** the report. 我被這個報導嚇了一跳。

▶ We were <u>amazed</u> **at** his strength. 他的力量令我們大吃一驚。

▶ I'm <u>angry</u> **at** what you did just now. 我為你剛才所做的事感到生氣。

▶ He is <u>bad</u> **at** writing essays. 他不擅於寫作文。

▶ They are <u>clever</u> **at** weaving baskets. 他們擅長編籃子。

▶ We were <u>disappointed</u> **at** not getting the tickets. 我們對沒有拿到票而感到失望。

▶ The lawyer was <u>displeased</u> **at** the judgment. 這個律師對判決感到不滿。

▶ He is very <u>good</u> **at** mathematics. 他擅長數學。

▶ She is <u>good</u> **at** sewing clothes. 她擅長縫紉衣服。

▶ We are <u>pleased</u> **at** having won the debate. 我們很高興贏得辯論賽。

▶ She was <u>shocked</u> **at** his bad behavior. 他的不良行為使她大為震驚。

▶ I'm <u>surprised</u> **at** his bad temper. 我對他的壞脾氣感到驚訝。

FOR

fit **for** 適合

excellent **for** 對…極有助益

tough **for** 對…而言是棘手的

good **for** 對…有益

opportune **for** 適合

bad **for** 對…有害

competent **for** 能夠勝任

ready **for** 準備好

convenient **for** 對…是方便的

famous **for** 因…出名

anxious **for** 為…擔心

essential **for** 對…是不可或缺的

spoken **for** 已被人預定的

▶ This place is <u>famous</u> **for** its food. 這個地方以其食物而聞名。

▶ There is a house <u>available</u> **for** rent. 有一間房屋可供租用。

▶ Reading in a dim light is <u>bad</u> **for** your eyes. 在光線微弱的地方閱讀對你的眼睛有害。

▶ It is <u>correct</u> **for** you to call her "Aunt Sally." 你稱呼她莎莉姑媽是對的。

▶ It is <u>necessary</u> **for** us to keep fit. 我們必須保持健康。

▶ Milk is good **for** your health. 牛奶對你的健康有益。

▶ They are greedy **for** success. 他們渴望成功。

▶ The children are ready **for** dinner. 孩子們準備好要吃晚飯了。

▶ The goods are ready **for** packing. 這些貨物已經準備好可以包裝了。

▶ I'm sorry **for** hurting you. 很抱歉我傷害了你。

▶ They feel sorry **for** the blind child. 他們對那失明的小孩感到同情。

FROM

safe **from** 沒有…的危險	absent **from** 缺席
alienated **from** 與…疏離	different **from** 和…不同
aloof **from** 與…疏離	free **from** 免於
separate **from** 與…分離	

▶ He is absent **from** school today. 他今天缺課。

▶ My notebook is different **from** yours. 我的筆記本和你的不同。

▶ The prisoner has been set free **from** jail. 這個犯人已從監獄被釋放出來了。

▶ He is tired **from** walking such a long distance. 他因為走了這麼長的路而感到疲倦。

IN

abundant **in** 有豐富的…	adept **in** 擅於
inherent **in** 在…是固有的	disappointed **in** 對…失望
interested **in** 對…有興趣	prominent **in** 在…方面很傑出
different **in** …不同	expert **in** 對…很熟練

▶ They are different **in** appearance. 他們外貌不同。

▶ She was disappointed **in** her efforts to make peace. 她對她為議和所做的努力感到失望。

▶ The manager was interested **in** the plans. 經理對這些計畫有興趣。

▶ He was successful **in** his application for the job. 他成功地申請到那份工作。

OF

tired **of** 對…感到厭煩	fond **of** 喜歡
aware **of** 知道	proud **of** 對…感到驕傲
capable **of** 有…能力	envious **of** 羨慕
ignorant **of** 不知道	afraid **of** 害怕

ashamed **of** 為…感到羞恥   worthy **of** 值…

tolerant **of** 容忍   jealous **of** 嫉妒

characteristic **of** 有…的特性   full **of** 充滿

sure **of** 確定   conscious **of** 意識到

▶ She is <u>afraid **of**</u> the Alsatian dog. 她害怕這隻德國狼犬。

▶ He was <u>ashamed **of**</u> his behavior at the party. 他為自己在宴會中的行為感到羞恥。

▶ He is <u>certain **of**</u> his horse's winning the race. 他確信他的馬會贏得比賽。

▶ She is <u>confident **of**</u> her success in the examination. 她有信心她會考得很好。

▶ He is very <u>fond **of**</u> his nephew. 他很喜歡他的姪子。

▶ We are <u>fond **of**</u> eating mangoes. 我們喜歡吃芒果。

▶ At last he was <u>free **of**</u> debts. 最後他把債務還清。

▶ He is very <u>proud **of**</u> his prize-winning roses. 他非常以他得獎的玫瑰為榮。

▶ He was <u>jealous **of**</u> her success. 他嫉妒她的成功。

▶ We were <u>sure **of**</u> getting that contract. 我們相信會得到那份合約。

▶ She is <u>tired **of**</u> eating the same food every day. 她厭倦每天吃同樣的食物。

ON

drunk **on** 喝…醉了   keen **on** 對…很渴望

▶ They are <u>keen **on**</u> starting the work. 他們非常渴望開始工作。

TO

tempted **to** 很想要做…   common **to** 共有的

applicable **to** 適用於   prone **to** 有…的傾向

subject **to** 易遭受   indifferent **to** 對…漠不關心

addicted **to** 沉溺於   accustomed **to** 習慣於

likely **to** 可能，易於   obliged **to** 感激

superior **to** 比…優越   impossible **to** 對…是不可能的

fatal **to** 對…是致命的   equal **to** 能勝任

difficult **to** 對…是困難的   senior **to** 比…年長

devoted **to** 致力於

▶ He is very <u>attentive **to**</u> his wife. 他很體貼他的妻子。

▶ The car will be available **to** you in an hour. 一個小時後你就可以用這車子了。

▶ Sleep is necessary **to** us all. 睡眠對我們所有人是必要的。

▶ We are used ___ to getting up at six in the morning. 我們習慣早上六點起床。

WITH

angry **with** 對⋯生氣	busy **with** 忙著
acquainted **with** 與⋯熟識	clever **with** 善於使用
disappointed **with** 對⋯感到失望	pleased **with** 對⋯感到滿意
ill **with** 患（病）	

▶ We were angry **with** her for being late. 我們氣她遲到。

▶ She is busy **with** her work. 她忙著她的工作。

▶ He is clever **with** his hands. 他的手很巧。

▶ He is disappointed **with** her performance. 他對她的表演感到失望。

▶ He is very free **with** his money. 他花錢毫不吝惜。

▶ She is very friendly **with** him. 她和他非常友好。

▶ He is dissatisfied **with** his present job. 他對目前的工作不滿意。

▶ His father is pleased **with** the report card. 他的父親對他的成績單很滿意。

小練習

請在空格中填入合適的介系詞。

1. His opinion of that piece of woodwork is different _____ yours.

2. We were disappointed _____ not getting the contract.

3. I am angry _____ what he said about my hair.

4. Many of the girls are keen _____ studying Japanese, but few of them are interested _____ studying French.

5. Although she was very fond _____ her nieces, she was shocked _____ their bad manners.

6. My sister is good _____ history. She never seems to get tired _____ the subject.

7. He is dissatisfied _____ his present job. He wants to leave, but he isn't sure _____ getting another job.

8. Smoking is bad _____ your health. You should be ashamed _____ your half-hearted

efforts to give up the habit.

9. The waiters were very attentive _____ his requests, so he was very satisfied _____ the service.

10. We were not successful _____ persuading her not to be so displeased _____ her son.

11. We were amazed _____ his skill in judo, but now he's just a fat guy because he is too busy _____ his work.

☞ 更多相關習題請見本章應用練習 Part 4。

6-5 動詞 + 介系詞 + 名詞

ABOUT	
walk **about** the streets 在街頭遊蕩	be **about** five pages 大約五頁
be **about** two o'clock 大約兩點	ask **about** someone 詢問關於某人
talk **about** something 談論某事	

ABOVE	
fly **above** the trees 在樹上飛	look **above** him 往他上方看
cost **above** ten dollars 花費超過 10 元	rise **above** the mark 升到記號以上

ACROSS	
live **across** the road 住在路的另一邊	run **across** the field 跑過田野
come **across** someone 偶遇某人	

AFTER	
come **after** someone 緊跟著某人	go **after** someone 追逐某人
start **after** one o'clock 在一點後出發	retire **after** forty years 在四十年後退休
look **after** a baby 照顧嬰兒	talk **after** the show 在表演後交談

AGAINST	
knock **against** someone 撞到某人	be **against** the plan 反對這計畫
race **against** someone 和某人賽跑	struggle **against** poverty 努力脫離貧窮
lean **against** something 倚靠某物	warn **against** something 告誡不要做某事
go **against** the law 違法	fight **against** someone 與某人打架

rise **against** someone 奮起反抗某人

ALONG

run **along** the road 沿著路跑

AMONG

walk **among** the flowers 在花叢中走 decide **among** themselves 他們自己做決定

choose **among** the dresses 在這些衣服中選擇

AROUND

stand **around** you 站在你旁邊 run **around** the streets 在街上到處跑

gather **around** someone 聚集在某人的周圍 go **around** the town 在鎮上到處走

revolve **around** the sun 繞著太陽旋轉

AS

work **as** a clerk 擔任職員 act **as** a lever 作為手段

serve **as** a warning 作為警告 treat **as** a criminal 當作罪犯

rise **as** one man 萬眾一心起來（做…）

AT

stay **at** a place 停留在一個地方 feel **at** ease 感到自由自在

be **at** war 戰時 laugh **at** someone/something 嘲笑某人／物

look **at** someone/something 看著某人／物

BEFORE

come **before** a judge 來到法官面前 wash **before** eating 吃之前清洗

stand **before** the teacher 站在老師面前 walk **before** someone 走在某人之前

finish **before** you 在你之前完成 bow **before** the king 向國王鞠躬

BEHIND

lag **behind** someone 落後在某人後面 hide **behind** something 藏在某物後面

look **behind** him 看他身後

BELOW

write **below** the line 在這條線下面寫 swim **below** the surface 在水面下游泳

be **below** average 在平均之下   stand **below** the window 在窗子下站著

live **below** this floor 住在下一層樓   act **below** his age 舉止與他的年齡不相稱

flow **below** the ground 在地下面流動 creep **below** the wires 在電纜下爬行

BESIDE

sit **beside** him 坐在他旁邊   stand **beside** me 站在我旁邊

walk **beside** the line 貼著線走   be **beside** the point 談話離題

BETWEEN

walk **between** two persons 在兩人之間行走 share **between** us 我們彼此分享

choose **between** the two 在兩者之間選擇 sit **between** us 坐在我們中間

come **between** one and two o'clock 在一點到二點之間來

is **between** two and three years old 介於二到三歲之間

BY

abide **by** the rules 遵守規章   stand **by** his friend 站在他的朋友旁邊

travel **by** bus 坐公車旅行   pass **by** a village 經過一個村莊

paint **by** hand 手繪   win **by** two points 以兩分獲勝

DOWN

come **down** the hill 下山丘   pour **down** the drain 從排水管中傾注而下

glance **down** the lists 瀏覽名冊   fall **down** the steps 摔下樓梯

lay **down** their weapons 放下他們的武器

FOR

walk **for** kilometers 走數公里   look **for** something 尋找某物

come **for** dinner 來吃晚餐   shout **for** joy 高興地歡呼

change **for** something 為某事做改變 beg **for** something 乞求某物

start **for** home 動身回家

FROM

borrow **from** someone 向某人借   sail **from** the harbor 從港口出航

dangle **from** the roof 掛在屋頂上   escape **from** those guards 逃離那些警衛

watch **from** the window 從窗戶看過去	awake **from** sleep 從睡眠中醒來

IN

return **in** January 在一月返回	indulge **in** gambling 沈迷於賭博
be **in** distress 貧困	answer **in** ten minutes 在十分鐘之內回答
bear **in** mind 記住	live **in** luxury 生活奢華
invest **in** a business 投資生意	assist **in** the work 協助工作
run **in** the race 賽跑	come **in** disguise 化裝而來

INTO

go **into** the shop 走進商店	look **into** the matter 調查這事
burst **into** laughter 突然開始大笑	turn **into** water 變成水
get **into** trouble 陷入麻煩	rush **into** a room 衝進一個房間
bite **into** an apple 咬一個蘋果	crawl **into** a hole 爬進一個洞
gaze **into** the darkness 注視黑暗	jump **into** the pool 跳進水池

NEAR

live **near** the school 住在學校附近	be **near** midnight 接近午夜
stand **near** me 站在我附近	get **near** retirement age 接近退休年齡
go **near** a car 走近一輛車	keep **near** someone 保持在某人附近

OF

speak **of** something 談到某事	rob **of** something 搶東西
be **of** superior quality 品質優良	taste **of** vinegar 有醋的味道

OFF

break **off** the friendship 停止友誼	keep **off** the grass 禁止踐踏草坪
jump **off** the wall 從牆上跳下來	finish **off** a job 完成工作
turn **off** the tap 關上水龍頭	switch **off** the fan 關掉電扇
take **off** your shoes 脫掉你的鞋子	wash **off** a mark 洗掉記號
saw **off** the jagged edge 鋸掉參差不齊的邊緣	

ON

float **on** the water 漂浮在水上	lean **on** the walking stick 倚著拐杖

talk **on** a subject/topic 針對一個主題做演講	be **on** fire 著火
act **on** advice 依建議行事	get **on** a bus 上公車

▶ They were **on** the air for half an hour yesterday. 昨天他們廣播了半個小時。

OVER

read **over** the notes 略讀筆記	quarrel **over** something 為某事爭吵
climb **over** the wall 爬過牆	fall **over** the cliff 掉落懸崖
argue **over** something 為某事爭論	talk **over** a subject 討論一個主題
go **over** the assignment 檢查作業	ponder **over** an idea 思考一個主意

THROUGH

shine **through** the fog 穿過霧發亮	go **through** the lessons 反覆研究這些課
seep **through** the ground 滲出地表	break **through** the wall 衝破牆
walk **through** the door 穿過門	search **through** my room 搜尋我的房間
run **through** the woods 跑過樹林	
peer **through** binoculars 透過雙筒望遠鏡盯著看	
succeed **through** hard work 透過努力工作而成功	

TO

travel **to** a place 到一個地方旅行	speak **to** someone 對某人講話
send **to** prison 被監禁	fasten **to** an object 固定在一個物體上
refer **to** someone 提到某人	go **to** war 參戰
take...**to** heart 對…耿耿於懷	put **to** sea 啟航
attach **to** something 附加在某物上	put...**to** sleep 麻醉…；哄…入睡

▶ You won't come **to** any harm with him beside you. 有他在你身邊你不會有任何危險。

▶ The murderer was finally brought **to** justice. 這個殺人犯最後被繩之以法。

▶ He rose **to** his feet when she came in. 當她進來的時候，他站了起來。

▶ They drank **to** the success of the expedition. 他們為探險成功乾杯。

▶ They put **to** sea as quickly as possible. 他們儘快地出航了。

TOWARD

come **toward** evening 接近傍晚	crawl **toward** the door 朝向門爬去

save **toward** a holiday 為假期而存錢

drive **toward** a place 朝一個地方開車過去

walk **toward** the sea 向大海走

contribute **toward** a fund 捐款給基金會

move **toward** the food 向食物移動

run **toward** someone 跑向某人

lean **toward** something（見解等）傾向於

UNDER

be **under** age 未成年

work **under** someone 在某人手下工作

be **under** orders 奉命

hide **under** the bed 躲在床下

be **under** his protection 在他的保護之下

take **under** an hour 花不到一小時

UP

walk **up** a hill 走上山丘

dig **up** the plant 挖出植物

come **up** the road 走上那條路

climb **up** a tree 爬上樹

live **up** the road 住在前面路上

UPON

lean **upon** a stick 倚靠著手杖

meditate **upon** a topic 沈思一個主題

agree **upon** an idea 同意一個想法

WITH

write **with** a pen 用筆寫字

quarrel **with** someone 與某人爭吵

play **with** something 玩某物

stain **with** ink 被墨水沾污

fight **with** someone 和某人打架

speak **with** an accent 帶著口音講話

laugh **with** joy 高興地大笑

cook **with** oil 用油煮

come **with** someone 與某人一起來

compete **with** someone 與某人競爭

WITHIN

pay **within** a week 在一週內支付

hide **within** a shell 躲在殼裡

finish **within** an hour 在一個小時內完成

be **within** my power 在我的能力範圍內

come **within** sight 來到視線範圍內

keep **within** the limit 不超出限制

talk **within** reason 合情合理地講話

remain **within** the premises 符合前提下

WITHOUT

> walk **without** help 在沒有輔助的情況下走路　beat **without** mercy 毫無憐憫地打

6-6 名詞 + 介系詞 + 名詞

ABOUT	
discussion **about** something 討論某事	enthusiasm **about** something 對某事的熱情
book **about** animals 關於動物的書	lecture **about** behavior 對行為的告誡

ABOVE	
person **above** criticism 無可挑剔的人	person **above** you 優於你的人
test **above** your ability 超過你能力的測驗	something **above** my notice 我沒注意到的事

AFTER	
hour **after** hour 一小時接著一小時	thirst **after** fame 對成名的渴望
day **after** day 日復一日	painting **after** Picasso 仿畢卡索的畫

AGAINST	
protest **against** the bill 對這法案的抗議	race **against** time 和時間賽跑
struggle **against** greed 面對貪念的掙扎	evidence **against** someone 不利某人的證據

AT	
attendance **at** the meeting 出席會議	expert **at** riding 騎馬的高手
child **at** play 玩耍的孩子	skill **at** archery 箭術方面的技能
disgust **at** the sight 一看見就感到厭惡	

BETWEEN
compromise **between** two persons 兩人之間的妥協
difference **between** two things 兩件事的差別
resemblance **between** two persons 兩人間的相似
distinction **between** two things 兩件事的區別

BY	
painting **by** Van Gogh 梵谷的畫	journey **by** night 夜晚的旅行

house **by** the river 河邊的房子	Australian **by** birth 土生的澳洲人
side **by** side 肩並肩地	one **by** one 一個一個地
tree **by** a house 房子旁的樹	

FOR

formula **for** happiness 快樂的不變公式	genius **for** doing something 做某事的才能
capacity **for** work 工作能力	desire **for** something 渴望某物
esteem **for** a person 尊重某人	concern **for** a person 關懷某人

▶ She repeated everything he said, <u>word **for** word</u>. 她把他說的話逐字地重複一遍。

FROM

quotation **from** the play 來自這戲劇的引言	departure **from** the ordinary 不平凡
permission **from** a person 某人的許可	answer **from** someone 某人的回答

IN

pioneer **in** medicine 醫學的先驅者	belief **in** religion 宗教信仰
skill **in** weaving 紡織技能	monopoly **in** a trade 貿易壟斷
delight **in** work 樂於工作	graduate **in** Economics 讀經濟學的畢業生
superiority **in** intellect 智力高	specialist **in** ear trouble 耳疾的專家
trust **in** someone 信任某人	discrepancy **in** a report 報告中不一致之處
experience **in** climbing 攀登的經驗	flaw **in** your theory 你的理論中的缺點
expert **in** cooking 烹飪專家	

OF

souvenir **of** a country 國家的紀念品	product **of** this place 這個地方的產品
specimen **of** a flower 花的採集樣品	touch **of** reality 現實風格
combination **of** colors 顏色的混合	flood **of** tears 大量的淚水
version **of** a story 故事的版本	envy **of** a person 羨慕的對象
taste **of** success 成功的滋味	march **of** time 時間的進行
acceptance **of** a job 接受一項工作	discharge **of** a person 解聘某人
advantage **of** someone 某人的優點	breach **of** promise 違反承諾

ON

advice **on** a subject 對某一主題的建議	agreement **on** an issue 對問題的協議
emphasis **on** education 注重教育	mercy **on** a person 憐憫某人
debate **on** a topic 對某一題目的辯論	influence **on** someone 對某人的影響
outlook **on** life 人生觀	

OVER

triumph **over** someone 戰勝某人	power **over** someone 對某人的影響力
command **over** a regiment 對軍團的命令	a quarrel **over** something 為某事爭吵
cloth **over** the table 桌上的桌巾	

TO

objection **to** something 反對某事	prey **to** doubts 為懷疑所折磨
sequel **to** a story 故事的續集	solution **to** a problem 解決問題的方法
reaction **to** the news 對新聞的回應	

▶ He chose the path **to** glory. 他選擇通往光榮之路。

TOWARD

a trend **toward** long hair 留長髮的趨勢	a feeling **toward** a person 對某人的感覺
hostility **toward** someone 對某人的敵意	a walk **toward** a place 朝某地走去

UPON

row **upon** row 一列又一列	limitation **upon** the time 時間的限制

WITH

trouble **with** someone 和某人之間的紛爭	feud **with** a tribe 與一個部落的世仇
struggle **with** something 為某事奮鬥	business **with** a company 與一家公司的生意
patience **with** someone 對某人的耐心	

小練習

請在空格中填入合適的介系詞。

1. His concern _____ the welfare _____ the poor has won him much popularity _____ people.

2. My sister has a great deal _____ talent _____ ballet dancing and has made quite a

name _____ herself.

3. A bully always takes advantage _____ the weak, but is usually timid _____ the face _____ danger.

4. He looked _____ the magazines _____ indifference and said that he had no intention _____ buying any.

5. That man is _____ arrest _____ armed robbery. The police have enough proof _____ him to put him in jail _____ ten years.

6. I asked her _____ her opinion _____ the book. She said that she did not enjoy it as there were several flaws _____ the plot _____ the story.

7. No one noticed his absence _____ the meeting. He has shown no interest _____ the affairs _____ the club for some time.

8. We paid _____ the television set _____ advance and the salesman has given us a receipt _____ it.

9. They have no more patience _____ him because he doesn't pay any attention _____ them and they seem to have no influence _____ him.

10. Mrs. Brown is _____ a diet, and every member _____ her family is showing a lot of consideration _____ her.

11. Dr. Shaw is a specialist _____ heart disease. My uncle has shown great improvement _____ his condition since he went _____ treatment.

12. The plane will arrive _____ schedule; I can assure you _____ that. I have flown _____ time _____ time _____ that country _____ business, and I have no complaints _____ the airline service at all.

13. Her strong independence _____ her wealthy father and her broad outlook _____ life have made her a much-respected woman _____ both the rich and the poor.

6-7 形容詞＋介系詞＋名詞

ABOUT	
glad **about** something 為某事而高興	serious **about** something 認真看待某事
suspicious **about** a person 懷疑某人	excited **about** something 為某事感到興奮
mad **about** the movie star 為影星而瘋狂	disturbed **about** something 為某事心亂

clear **about** a fact 確信一項事實	angry **about** the delay 對延誤感到生氣
upset **about** the noise 對噪音感到心煩	certain **about** his ambition 確定他的野心
careful **about** his clothes 注意他的衣著	

AT

present **at** a meeting 出席會議	pleased **at** the result 對結果感到滿意
expert **at** doing something 對某事很專精	shocked **at** your action 對你的行動感到震驚

▶ Their house is close **at** hand, so we can go over whenever we like.

他們家就在附近，所以我們想過去就過去。

FOR

ready **for** action 準備好行動	famous **for** the song 因這首歌而出名
sufficient **for** you 對你而言足夠	satisfactory **for** the job 適合這工作
fit **for** work 適合工作	hungry **for** affection 渴望感情
suitable **for** someone 適合某人	grateful **for** something 對某事感到感激
available **for** use 可供使用	responsible **for** something 對某事負責

FROM

safe **from** danger 沒有危險	aloof **from** classmates 疏遠同學
free **from** duty 免稅	different **from** something 與某事不同
absent **from** school 曠課	distinct **from** something 與某事有區別

IN

prominent **in** society 在社會中傑出	peculiar **in** one's habit 特別的習慣
weak **in** character 性格軟弱	specific **in** your aim 你的目標明確
inherent **in** a person 某人與生俱來的	generous **in** your action 你行為慷慨
brilliant **in** something 在某方面很傑出	successful **in** his work 他的工作很成功
flawless **in** writing 在寫作方面毫無瑕疵	abundant **in** fruit 盛產水果
disinterested **in** a subject 對某科目沒興趣	adept **in** carving 在雕刻方面很熟練

OF

worthy **of** notice 值得注意	sick **of** his hair 看他的頭髮看到很煩
expressive **of** his joy 表現出他的喜悅	short **of** money 缺錢

appreciative **of** the kindness 感激好心	confident **of** success 有信心成功
careless **of** his health 疏忽他的健康	cautious **of** his steps 留心他的步伐

ON

clear **on** a point 在某點上很清楚的

TO

similar **to** something 類似某物	superior **to** someone 優於某人
junior **to** someone 比某人年幼	applicable **to** this case 適用於這個情況
prone **to** illness 容易生病的	blind **to** his faults 對他的錯誤視而不見
hostile **to** someone 對某人有敵意	true **to** his word 忠於他所說的話
faithful **to** his school 忠於他的學校	obedient **to** someone 服從某人
similar **to** mine 和我的類似	

WITH

careless **with** his money 他用錢不小心	heavy **with** sadness 因悲傷而感到沉重
satisfied **with** the results 對結果感到很滿意	
disappointed **with** his work 對他的工作感到失望	

6-8 介系詞 + 名詞 + 介系詞

AGAINST

against the will **of** 違反…的意願

▶ They passed the bill **against** the will **of** people. 他們通過違背民意的法案。

AT

at the speed **of** 以…速度	**at** the mercy **of** 任…擺佈
at war **with** 和…交戰	**at** the risk **of** 冒著…的危險
at the rate **of** 以…的速率	**at** the cost **of** 以…為代價

BESIDE

beside oneself **with**... 某人情緒極度…

BY

by way **of** 經由	**by** means **of** 藉著
by the name **of** 名叫	**by** reason **of** 由於

FOR

for fear **of** 唯恐	**for** lack **of** 因缺少
for the good **of** 為了…的利益	**for** the sake **of** 為了

IN

in doubt **of** 懷疑	**in** favor **of** 有利於
in addition **to** 除…之外	**in** case **of** 萬一
in aid **of** 為了幫助	**in** consequence **of** 由於
in charge **of** 負責	**in** succession **to** 繼承
in company **with** 和…一起	**in** defense **of** 防衛
in league **with** 與…聯合	**in** accordance **with** 根據
in awe **of** 敬畏	**in** command **of** 控制
in comparison **with** 跟…比較	**in** readiness **for** 準備好
in conflict **with** 和…衝突	**in** agreement **with** 與…一致
in store **for** 即將發生	**in** spite **of** 儘管

▶ The soldiers fought bravely <u>in the face of</u> great difficulties.

　　這些士兵在面臨極大困難時英勇作戰。

▶ We always keep <u>in touch with</u> each other. 我們一直相互保持聯繫。

▶ That small boy is next <u>in succession to</u> the throne. 那個小男孩是王位的優先繼承者。

ON

on the basis **of** 基於	**on** the edge **of** 在…的邊緣
on the chance **of** 懷著…的希望	**on** behalf **of** 代表
on the strength **of** 基於	**on** a level **with** 與…同一程度
on the part **of** 就…而言	**on** the way **to** 在去…的路上
on receipt **of** 收到…時	**on** the eve **of** 在…的前夕
on the verge **of** 瀕臨	

▶ She is **on** the verge **of** a nervous breakdown. 她瀕臨精神崩潰。

▶ I was **on** the point **of** leaving when he appeared. 當他出現的時候，我正要離去。

OUT OF

out of touch **with** 與…失去聯繫	**out of** patience **with** 對…失去耐心
out of the reach **of** 超出…的可及範圍	**out of** respect **for** 出於對…的尊重

TO

to the satisfaction **of** 讓…滿意

UNDER

under the name **of** 以…的名義	**under** the eye **of** 在…的監視下
under the command **of** 在…的指揮下	**under** the cover **of** 在…的掩護下

UP TO

up to one's elbows **in** 忙於

WITH

with respect **to** 關於	**with** the intention **of** 以…為目的
with the exception **of** 除…之外	**with** reference **to** 關於
with an eye **to** 著眼於	**with** the compliments **of** 某人向你致意
with regard **to** 關於	

▶ He visited her many times, **with** a view **to** marriage. 他拜訪她許多次，期望能和她結婚。

WITHIN

within the limit **of** 在限制內	**within** the bounds **of** 在權限內
within the sound **of** 在可聽到的範圍內	

WITHOUT

without regard **to** 不考慮

6-9 介系詞片語與慣用語

ABOUT

▶ What **about** stopping here for a cup of coffee? 我們在這停一下喝杯咖啡如何？

▶ Stop beating **about** the bush, and tell me what happened!

　不要拐彎抹角，告訴我到底發生了什麼事！

ABOVE

above water 在水面上	**above** reproach 無可挑剔
above average 在平均之上	

AFTER

after dinner 晚飯後	**after** four o'clock 四點以後
All of us can dance, **after** a fashion. 我們所有的人都能跳一點舞。	

AGAINST

cry out **against** 大聲反對	rub up **against** 摩擦
stand out **against** 堅持反對	

AT

at the top 在頂部	**at** lunch 在午餐時候
at the bottom 在底部	**at** home 在家
at first 起初	**at** full speed 全速地

▶ Don't worry; help is **at** hand. 不要擔心；救援就快到了。

▶ She kept them **at** arm's length all through her visit.

　在她的整個拜訪期間，她與他們保持距離。

▶ She is always **at** odds with the rest of us. 她總是和我們其他人不一致。

▶ He was **at** loose ends, so I called him over to my house. 他沒事做，所以我叫他過來我家。

BEHIND

behind time 遲到

BELOW

below average 平均以下	**below** the surface 在表面底下

BEYOND

beyond reason 無理由地	**beyond** the limit 超過限制

BY

by the side of 在…的旁邊　　　　　　by accident 偶然

by post 用郵寄的方式　　　　　　　do well by someone 善待某人

▶ All the children learned the lesson **by** heart. 所有的小孩都把這一課背下來。

▶ He lives **by** his pen and not **by** his sword. 他並沒有從軍，而是靠寫作維生。

FOR

make up **for** 補償　　　　　　　　stand in **for** 暫時代替

stand up **for** 支持，維護　　　　　**for** a long time 長時間

for long 長久

▶ Many people seem to go in **for** golf nowadays. 現今許多人似乎喜歡打高爾夫球。

▶ They stood up **for** the rights of women. 他們維護婦女的權利。

▶ They are leaving this place **for** good. 他們要永遠地離開這個地方。

▶ I would have failed but **for** his help. 要不是他幫忙，我早就失敗了。

▶ She made up **for** the day she was absent by working overtime.
　　她加班來彌補她沒來上班的那一天。

▶ He had plenty of food **for** thought when his friend was arrested.
　　當他的朋友被逮捕時，引起他的深思。

▶ Stand up **for** yourself, or you will get bullied. 維護你自己的權利，否則你會被人欺負。

▶ When the mayor is away, the deputy mayor stands in **for** him.
　　當市長不在的時候，副市長暫時代替他的工作。

FROM

from the first 起初

▶ I was feeling far **from** glad to be home again. 回到家裡，我一點也不覺得高興。

▶ Her house is a home away **from** home for us. 她家是像我們自家一樣舒適的地方。

▶ Apart **from** such petty disturbances, his visit was a peaceful one.
　　除了這樣的小騷動之外，他的訪問是和平的。

IN

in disguise 偽裝　　　　　　　　**in** line with 與…一致

in trouble 處於困境　　　　　　　be wrapped up **in** 醉心於

▶ **In** time, you will be able to do it all by yourself. 遲早你會有能力全靠自己去做它。

▶ The matter is **in** their hands now; I can do nothing about it.

這件事目前在他們的掌控中；我無計可施。

OF

make fun **of** 嘲笑　　　　　　　　　　　take care **of** 照顧

take note **of** 注意

▶ We have run short **of** matches. Can you buy some on your way back?

我們的火柴快用完了，你回來時能買一些嗎？

▶ They made a point **of** always being punctual. 他們認為永遠堅持準時是很重要的。

▶ All **of** a sudden, the rain started. 突然間開始下起雨來。

▶ He will be a wealthy man when he comes **of** age. 當他成年的時候，他將是一個富有的人。

▶ I haven't seen Robert or Richard **of** late. 最近以來我沒有見到羅伯特或李察。

▶ People **of** old had different problems from people **of** today. 古人有不同於現代人的問題。

▶ University life may make a man **of** him. 大學生活可使他成為男子漢。

▶ I can't make anything **of** this message. It must be in code.

我完全不懂這個訊息的意思，它一定是用密碼發送的。

▶ He is a man **of** note in this district. 他是這個地區有名的人物。

▶ That girl is **of** a wealthy family. 那個女孩出自富裕的家庭。

OFF

off the ground 離開地面　　　　　　　　**off** duty 下班

off the mark 不正確的

▶ These policemen are **off** duty now. 這些警察現在下班了。

▶ Be careful! He will take advantage of you if you are **off** your guard.

小心！如果你不提防，他就會占你便宜。

▶ I wonder what's wrong with the dog. It has been **off** its food recently.

我想知道這隻狗是怎麼回事，它最近不吃東西。

ON

on lease 以租借方式　　　　　　　　　　on fire 正在燃燒

on the contrary 反之　　　　　　　　　　lay a hand on 傷害

look down on 鄙視　　　　　　　　　　　fall back on 借助

go back **on** 違背

on time 準時

on foot 徒步

▶ What is **on** your mind? 你在擔心什麼？

▶ The doctor is **on** call both day and night. 這個醫生白天和晚上都隨時待命。

▶ Mr. Brown is **on** the line asking for you. 布朗先生打電話找你。

▶ There were a few people **on** the spot when he was arrested.

當他被逮捕時，有一些人在現場。

▶ **On** second thought, I had better wait here. 進一步考慮後，我最好在這裡等。

▶ Will you drop in **on** Mrs. Harper on the way? 你在途中會去探望哈波太太嗎？

▶ It would be better to have a few men **on** hand in case there is trouble.

最好找一些人隨同以防有麻煩。

▶ The joke was lost **on** John, who didn't even know what we were talking about.

約翰聽不懂那則笑話，他根本不知道我們在說什麼。

OUT OF

out of pity 出於同情

out of town 不在鎮上

pull **out of** 拔出

take a lot **out of** 使筋疲力盡

out of sight 從視線中消失

run **out of** 用光

talk **out of** 勸阻

▶ They backed **out of** the deal at the last minute. 他們在最後一刻取消這項交易。

▶ We ran **out of** food, so we had to turn back. 我們的食物吃光了，所以我們必須折回。

TO

to this day 直到今天

make up **to** 巴結

be up **to** 由…決定

tag on **to** 附上

run up **to** 高達

look up **to** 尊敬

put down **to** 把…歸因於

sit down **to** 坐下（做…）

take something **to** heart 認真關注

▶ The musician set the words **to** music. 這個音樂家為這些文字譜曲。

▶ He is generous **to** a fault. 他過份地慷慨。

▶ The children ate **to** their hearts' content. 這些小孩盡情地吃。

▶ We don't see eye **to** eye on this matter. 在這個事情上我們的看法不一致。

▶ I will not be a party **to** such an outrageous act. 我與如此無法無天的行為無關。

▶ Mary looks up **to** her brother for his help and advice.
  瑪麗尊敬她的哥哥，因為他幫她並給她建議。

▶ The curry is not **to** my taste. 這咖哩不合我的味口。

UNDER

under repair 修理中　　　　　　　　　　　**under** age 未成年

under cultivation 用來當作耕地

UP

▶ He made **up** his mind to become a poet. 他決心要成為詩人。

▶ The robber gave himself **up** at the nearest police station.
  這個搶匪在最近的警察局自首。

WITH

with ease 從容地　　　　　　　　　　　**with** reference to 關於…

get away **with** 逃脫　　　　　　　　　　　run off **with** 偷走

make away **with** 偷走　　　　　　　　　　make do **with** 湊合地用

put up **with** 忍受　　　　　　　　　　　　do away **with** 免於…

fall in **with** 贊同

▶ We fell in **with** their suggestion. 我們贊同他們的提議。

▶ She was laid up **with** a broken leg for a month. 她因為斷了一條腿而一個月臥床不起。

▶ They can't catch up **with** the work we have done. 他們無法趕上我們的工作進度。

WITHIN

within sight 視野之內　　　　　　　　　**within** hearing 聽得見的範圍內

within one's means 在某人的財力範圍內

WITHOUT

without effort 毫不費力　　　　　　　　**without** warning 沒有警告

without delay 立刻

Chapter 6　應用練習

PART 1

請在空格中填入合適的介系詞。

1. He took _____ his hat, pulled _____ his handkerchief, and mopped his forehead.

2. Classes will finish _____ seven o'clock, so I will meet you _____ a quarter past seven _____ the entrance _____ the school.

3. We bought some apples _____ the stall and waited _____ the bus.

4. The motor is worked _____ electricity and it pumps _____ water _____ a speed _____ 150 liters per minute.

5. They stayed _____ Disneyland _____ a day and then set out _____ home the next day.

6. He parked his bicycle _____ the gate.

7. A dog barked _____ him, but he was not afraid _____ it.

8. Would you like to go _____ a swim _____ the afternoon? We can go _____ car.

9. I bought this handbag _____ ten dollars _____ a shop _____ Orchard Road.

10. Henry was excused _____ not taking part _____ the Big Walk because _____ ill health.

11. "Don't say anything bad _____ people. It reflects _____ yourself," he advised.

12. Peter wanted to row out _____ the island, but his sister was not _____ favor _____ his plan.

13. They ran _____ the beach, shouting _____ delight.

14. He ran along the street to look _____ something which had fallen _____ that man's backpack.

15. Mr. Brown packed a few articles _____ his suitcase and left hurriedly.

16. The stream flowed _____ an orchard to join the main river a kilometer away _____ town.

PART 2

請在空格中填入合適的介系詞。

1. He was very specific _____ the instructions.

2. I leaned _____ the wall and tried to concentrate _____ the problem.

3. This boy is very good _____ arithmetic. He has inherited this talent _____ his father.

4. He is annoyed _____ me. He says that my failure is a great disappointment _____ him.

5. She was delighted _____ the present I gave her _____ her birthday last week.

6. Are you satisfied _____ this, or would you like to ask _____ some more?

7. The misunderstanding _____ them is getting serious. They are feeling more and more hostile _____ each other.

8. The convict escaped _____ prison, but he was captured _____ the police within a few days.

9. Is she familiar _____ this type of work? If she isn't, we must find something she is more fit _____ .

10. He took credit _____ everything even though we had carried out all the preparations _____ the occasion.

11. He congratulated Peter _____ his success _____ the examinations.

12. They were very keen _____ sports and emphasized athletics as essential _____ education.

13. He had no intention _____ coming back. He had taken his suitcase packed _____ all his clothes. His important papers were also missing _____ the drawer where he usually kept them.

14. I am hopeful _____ my chances _____ passing the examinations. I have been concentrating _____ my studies for many months.

15. The contrast _____ the two sisters is very great. Nancy is keen _____ music and literature, while Susan is more interested _____ outdoor sports and games. Nancy's taste _____ clothes is also entirely different _____ Susan's.

PART 3

請在空格中填入合適的介系詞。

1. I do not like to intrude _____ your privacy.

2. You should rely _____ your hard work.

3. Augustus reigned over the Roman Empire _____ 27 B.C. _____ 14 A.D.

4. She doesn't agree _____ us _____ that decision. Nevertheless, she has agreed to carry _____ our instructions.

5. He is a man endowed _____ a strong capacity _____ business affairs.

6. He impressed _____ them that hard work and perseverance are indispensable _____ success _____ life.

7. He was found guilty _____ murder and was subsequently sentenced _____ death.

8. The hippopotamus subsists chiefly _____ aquatic plants, but there are times when it looks _____ food _____ the land.

9. _____ the eleventh hour, she retired _____ the competition, leaving the field open _____ her rivals.

10. I was obliged _____ the stranger _____ his kindness _____ helping me when I was _____ a bad situation.

11. The clerk thought _____ a way to make himself richer _____ 30,000 dollars. However, he failed _____ his plan.

12. She was born _____ humble parents _____ a small village _____ the border.

13. They argued _____ a trivial matter and are not _____ speaking terms _____ each other now.

PART 4

請在空格中填入合適的介系詞。

1. My mother is good _____ cooking as well as at making clothes.

2. She is very proud _____ her musical talents. She is very eager _____ giving a piano recital at the Town Hall on Friday.

3. We feel sorry _____ her. Although we are friendly _____ her, there is nothing that we can do to help her.

4. He is busy _____ all his homework. He is disappointed _____ not being able to help us.

5. We are tired _____ staying at home in the evenings. We are very excited _____ our trip to Sunshine Isle, which is famous _____ its beaches.

6. She is very fond _____ dancing. Her style of dancing is very different _____ yours.

7. They are used _____ working without the fans on. It isn't necessary _____ you to switch them on.

8. We are getting ready _____ the debate this week. We are quite sure _____ winning it.

9. He is not very confident _____ success in the business until he is free _____ all his debts.

10. The child is very smart, and the teacher is very pleased _____ him for being so interested _____ his studies.

11. He is very keen _____ working his own way through the university. His parents are very worried _____ his ideas.

12. Everyone was surprised _____ his refusal to run for election again as president of the society. He said that he was afraid _____ some members' being jealous _____ his position.

PART 5

請在空格中填入合適的介系詞。

1. His greed _____ money made him appear false even _____ his best friend.

2. She was _____ the verge _____ despair when help arrived.

3. His version _____ the story is completely different _____ mine.

4. Doctors often discourage us _____ smoking as it is injurious _____ health.

5. His doctor warned him _____ smoking, but it was hard _____ him to give _____ the habit as he has been addicted _____ it for a long time.

6. That merchant was sued _____ breach _____ contract. He was fined a sum _____ two thousand dollars.

7. Don't say a word _____ anyone. Secrecy is vital _____ the success _____ our plan.

8. Be careful _____ the man if you are doing business _____ him. He is capable _____ the meanest tricks.

9. Although she was not fit _____ work yet, she insisted _____ going _____ the office.

10. We are not envious _____ his promotion, but we are _____ the idea of his being promoted _____ his superior.

11. Randy is weak _____ all his subjects. He is now studying _____ the guidance _____ a tutor.

12. At first, he refused to agree _____ the changes that we proposed _____ the plan, but he finally yielded _____ our persuasion.

13. He differs _____ me _____ this matter, but we are _____ agreement _____ all the other issues.

14. If you are sympathetic _____ our cause, could you please speak _____ the manager _____ it? We are quite nervous _____ meeting him ourselves.

15. The teacher warned him _____ being negligent _____ his work, but he paid no attention _____ her words. His failure _____ the examination made him feel sorry _____ ignoring her.

PART 6

請選擇合適的介系詞填入空格中。

1. She returned the package _____ (*to; at*) the postman.

2. The policeman went _____ (*to; by*) the house and took the gang _____ (*with; by*) surprise.

3. He snatched the gold chain _____ (*from; away*) the lady's neck.

4. Traffic was held up _____ (*in; on*) several places _____ (*with; by*) broken branches _____ (*in; on*) the road.

5. Please show her the way _____ (*at; to*) the town library.

6. I'll meet you _____ (*on; at*) the 'Oasis' snack bar _____ (*at; in*) half an hour.

7. The bridge _____ (*on; at*) River Road was washed away _____ (*with; by*) the floods.

8. He paid ten dollars _____ (*to; for*) the box of chocolates.

9. He fell _____ (*from; on*) his bicycle and landed _____ (*with; in*) the muddy pool.

10. She visited her friend _____ (*on; at*) the hospital _____ (*with; on*) the way home _____ (*at; from*) work.

11. Don't stand _____ (*beside; under*) a tree when it is raining.

12. She dipped the bottle _____ (*on; in*) the water.

13. He was not _____ (*in; on*) the plane bound _____ (*for; with*) Monaco.

14. She was writing a letter _____ (*to; with*) her brother _____ (*in; at*) Canada when I called.

PART 7

請選擇合適的介系詞填入空格中。

1. The play will be held _____ the Town Hall _____ the evening. (*at; in*)

2. She ran _____ the room _____ investigating where the noise had come _____ (*without; from; out of*)

3. She went _____ them _____ the waterfall yesterday. (*to; with*)

4. How many grams are there _____ a kilogram? Look _____ the answer _____ your book. (*in; in; up*)

5. He put _____ his glasses before writing _____ the sum _____ the blackboard. (*out; on; on*)

6. The helicopter landed _____ a clearing _____ the hospital. (*near; in*)

7. He looked _____ when the lizard dropped _____ the ceiling _____ his book. (*from; onto; up*)

8. We arrived _____ the airport _____ the evening. (*in; at*)

9. She used to sit _____ me _____ class. (*in; beside*)

10. Strong winds blow _____ the west coast of the island _____ May _____ October. (*to; from; along*)

11. She was _____ duty _____ the hospital last night. (*at; on*)

12. When they returned _____ the picnic _____ the waterfall, they found that their house had been broken _____ (*by; into; from*)

PART 8

請在空格中填入合適的介系詞。

1. Both _____ them were quarrelling _____ the toy, so their mother took it _____ them.

2. He was very surprised _____ the wide selection _____ things we could get _____ the shop.

3. He is so desperate _____ money that he has agreed to sell his watch to me _____ fifty dollars.

4. Those vegetables aren't fit _____ eating. Have you got any meat _____ the refrigerator?

5. The bridge _____ the Swift River is _____ repair _____ the moment. You'll have to go _____ another route.

6. I haven't heard _____ my friend _____ a long time. She is very lazy _____ writing letters.

7. It is very hard to ride your bicycle when the wind is blowing _____ you.

8. She is worried _____ the results _____ her test.

9. Don't argue _____ her _____ paying the bill. She is very generous _____ her money.

10. Who do you want to speak _____ ? I can call him _____ the phone _____ you.

11. He is very anxious to sell those shares _____ anyone willing to buy them.

12. What are you staring _____ ? Have you finished _____ your shopping?

13. We don't understand what she is upset _____ . We were getting ready _____ dinner when she came in and cried.

14. Who did you receive the gift _____ ?

PART 9

請在空格中填入合適的介系詞。

1. He locked himself _____ his room and even refused to come out _____ his meals.

2. The carpenter sawed the plank _____ half and tried to make a bench _____ _____ it.

3. I had forgotten all _____ the bags of cement in the backyard until he came _____ my room to remind me _____ them.

4. He lives _____ Clearwater Island, but he works _____ Lighthouse Bay. Every day, he has to travel _____ the mainland by ferry.

5. We had been traveling _____ more than two hours when we noticed a police car trying to catch up _____ us.

6. The countries agreed _____ an agreement to be signed _____ Paris as soon as

possible.

7. The boy escaped _____ his kidnappers _____ climbing _____ the window.

8. He dealt efficiently _____ the staff and promised them an improvement _____ their working conditions.

9. We were thinking _____ the day when one of the animals escaped _____ the zoo and caused a near panic _____ the town.

10. The victim was attacked _____ the head _____ behind. He has been unconscious _____ a few days.

11. The owner has put a "To Let" sign _____ the entrance _____ the mansion. We can have a look _____ the house if we like.

12. There's nothing to be afraid _____ . Why don't you ask Paul to go _____ you?

13. He stood _____ the middle _____ the road and waved his hands _____ every car that passed by.

14. Have you read the report _____ the newspaper? The men who hijacked the plane have been captured _____ the police.

15. I met a tourist _____ the ferry crossing _____ Pearl Island. He asked me the direction _____ his hotel.

PART 10

請選擇合適的介系詞填入空格中。

1. Will you explain _____ (*with; to*) him why Chinese New Year falls _____ (*in; on; for*) a different day every year?

2. They are planning a trip _____ (*on; to; around*) Singapore and Malaysia. They hope to stop _____ (*in; at; with*) Hong Kong _____ (*in; round; on*) the way.

3. The highest part _____ (*of; at*) the island is _____ (*by; in*) the center.

4. Usually vegetable farms are situated _____ (*in; on*) river valleys and _____ (*beside; against; in*) streams.

5. She ran _____ (*from; into*) the room and began to search frantically _____ (*for; in*) her drawer _____ (*in; for*) the documents.

6. He rolled his clothes _____ (on; into) a ball and threw them _____ (*at; on; into*) the laundry basket.

7. Something must have happened _____ (*in; for; to*) the child. He should have been home _____ (*from; till; by*) now.

8. The judge pronounced him guilty _____ (*by; of; in*) the crime and sentenced him _____ (*on; in; to*) five years' imprisonment.

9. These are the parts _____ (*from; in; of*) the model airplane. You fit them together according _____ (*from; to; on*) the instructions here.

10. Why don't you go ahead _____ (*of; with*) what you are doing? I will be concentrating _____ (*in; on*) my own work.

11. Mr. Baker went _____ (*out; to; back*) New Zealand _____ (*in; on*) Friday.

12. These flowers and rose plants are _____ (*on; from*) the Evergreen Nursery. Aunt Hilda brought them _____ (*for; with*) Mother.

13. The cat was _____ (*up; on*) the table when we came in.

14. He glanced _____ (*in; at*) the clock. It was time _____ (*to; on; for*) him to drive his sister _____ (*from; to; in*) the airport to catch the plane _____ (*to; by*) London.

PART 11

請從方框裡選擇合適的介系詞填入空格中。

at	about	above	of	after	against	among	before
across	by	down	in	behind	beside	below	between
from	around	on	for				

1. If he doesn't arrive _____ time, he will be _____ serious trouble.

2. Look _____ this photograph. The man sitting _____ the right has been convicted _____ murder.

3. The sun has gone down. It is too dark _____ you to walk home _____ yourself.

4. The equator lies _____ the Tropic _____ Cancer and the Tropic _____ Capricorn.

5. It is difficult _____ anyone to run _____ the wind.

6. They are traveling _____ the four o'clock train _____ Liverpool.

7. He worked _____ the crossword puzzle _____ going to bed.

8. His father was very disappointed _____ the boy's results. The grades _____ his

report card were all _____ average.

9. The blind girl thanked him _____ helping her _____ the road.

10. They talked _____ the theory _____ evolution _____ Charles Darwin.

11. He traveled _____ the world _____ ship last year.

12. The price _____ the refrigerator that you are pointing _____ is seven hundred dollars.

13. Look _____ the house while we are away. We'll be back _____ lunch.

14. The rich man did not want his sons to fight _____ themselves over his property _____ his death, so he divided it equally _____ the four of them.

15. We don't know anything _____ him. We found him _____ the bridge when we were passing _____ seven o'clock this morning.

PART 12

請從方框裡選擇合適的介系詞填入空格中。

off	over	out	past	since	through	to	into
under	until	up	with	without	within		

1. He has gone _____ food _____ yesterday.

2. By the time you make _____ your mind to go _____ the carnival, it will be over.

3. The soldiers went _____ the jungle after having gone _____ a month's training at their camp.

4. Dashing _____ _____ the room, he ran _____ the back of the garden and jumped _____ the fence.

5. The price of beef has gone up _____ last January.

6. The car crashed _____ the wall and burst _____ flames.

7. When he grows up, he wants to be a sailor and go _____ sea.

8. He accidentally fell _____ the river. That was why he was wet through when he came back at half _____ five.

9. You must return the money _____ a month, or else you will find yourself _____ your car.

10. He came _____ any delay and stayed _____ us until the ceremony was over.

11. We all agreed _____ his suggestion to search _____ every drawer in the chest until we found the missing key.

12. Mr. Green weighs _____ eighty-five kilograms, but he measures _____ 160 centimeters.

13. The girls cheered up when they found that they had not lost the game completely _____ the boys.

14. His mother was angry _____ him for not replying _____ his uncle's letter.

PART 13

請在空格中填入合適的介系詞。

1. This is a secret _____ you and me. We mustn't share it _____ anyone.

2. Littering the road is _____ the law. You could be fined _____ such an offence.

3. When he got _____ the taxi, his family rushed out _____ the house to welcome him.

4. We sat _____ the floor as there were no chairs _____ the room.

5. Mother is lying down _____ her room. She is having a rest before she continues _____ her work.

6. I have typed the letter _____ you.

7. Did you notice the dressings _____ his legs? He fell _____ his bicycle yesterday.

8. He walked away _____ a word.

9. We looked _____ the shop _____ almost an hour before we found what we wanted.

10. Sit _____ her while I pour a drink _____ her.

11. We were about to give _____ the search when we found the ring _____ the bushes.

12. The window broke _____ several pieces when he flung his shoe _____ it _____ a fit of anger.

13. This house was built _____ our grandfather _____ 1930. The floors are made _____ marble, and the house is full _____ antique pieces _____ furniture.

PART 14

請在空格中填入合適的介系詞。

1. _____ the last minute their plans fell through, so they had to stay home.

2. We talked our teacher _____ giving us a free period to prepare for the test.

3. The thief broke _____ Mr. Wilson's house and got away with 2,000 dollars in cash and jewelry.

4. That businessman tried to put me _____ with excuses, but I stuck _____ my demands.

5. Although the doctors have given _____ hope of her son's recovery, she believes that he will pull through.

6. He made _____ his villa to the orphanage and also set aside some money for its maintenance.

7. The missionary called _____ the natives to give _____ their rituals and traditional rites.

8. "Please stay to hear me _____," he said. "I'm sure that this idea of mine will work out."

9. The gardener hit _____ a good plan to get rid _____ the huge heaps of rubbish in the garden.

10. That man took us _____ completely. We thought that he was a gardener but he turned _____ to be a doctor.

PART 15

請在空格中填入合適的介系詞。

1. The monkey danced _____ tune _____ the music.

2. We were very excited _____ the thought _____ discovering a new place.

3. The marriage is not valid _____ the eyes _____ the law.

4. A man _____ the name _____ Tommy is looking for you.

5. Will we be _____ time _____ the opening ceremony?

6. We came here _____ the chance _____ meeting you.

7. Please accept this gift _____ a token _____ our friendship.

8. He was away _____ the time _____ his father's death.

9. You look very pale; you are _____ need _____ a long holiday.

10. They carried _____ the orders _____ accordance _____ his wishes.

11. The astonished boy was _____ a loss _____ words.

12. The poor man was _____ no mood _____ a joke.

13. Keep yourself _____ readiness _____ the match.

14. He has an independent spirit and doesn't like being _____ an obligation _____ anyone.

15. My father has been working for that company _____ more than ten years.

16. Benny has been afraid of water _____ that time he fell into the river.

PART 16

請在空格中填入介系詞 since 或 for 以完成句子。

1. They have been living here _____ 1970.

2. It hasn't rained _____ more than a month.

3. He has been ill _____ three days.

4. I have been wearing this watch _____ the age of twelve.

5. We have been waiting for you _____ more than an hour.

6. He has been working for the company _____ more than twenty years.

7. He has been sleeping _____ one o'clock this afternoon.

8. She has been playing the violin _____ the age of seven.

9. He has been driving a truck _____ ten years already.

10. They have been discussing the problem _____ several days.

11. She has been sewing that dress _____ yesterday.

12. The workmen have been repairing the roof _____ this morning.

13. I have not seen you _____ a long time. Tell me what you have been doing _____ the last time I saw you.

14. She has not had a holiday _____ years because she is always so busy.

15. I have been back _____ April, but I stayed with my aunt _____ the first week.

16. He has been delivering the newspaper to our house _____ several months.

17. The library was under construction. I have not been there _____ five months.

18. The little girl has been missing from her house _____ last Saturday. _____ then, her mother has been ill.

19. I haven't been there _____ last Christmas.

20. He has been sleeping _____ more than an hour.

21. You must sit down and study _____ at least two hours a day.

22. It had been raining _____ about half an hour.

23. _____ the last term holidays, they haven't had a chance to visit Uncle David.

24. He said that he hadn't eaten anything _____ last night.

25. _____ a moment, I thought that girl was Lucy.

26. There won't be another bus coming _____ at least half an hour, so we might as well walk home.

PART 17

請在空格中填入合適的介系詞。

1. I can't help you now; the matter is no longer _____ my hands.

2. I called _____ Lucy yesterday and told her the news.

3. I won't be able to come to the picnic, so don't count me _____ .

4. I took the stranger _____ a friend of mine and approached him.

5. They leaped _____ their feet and ran out of the room when the bell rang.

6. I'll stop _____ the shop on the way and collect all the groceries you want.

7. We were broken-hearted to learn that he was leaving the district _____ good.

8. Her favorite musical program will be _____ the air soon; that is why she is hurrying home.

9. We will have to count _____ their coming here as soon as possible.

10. I cannot stand people who always look down _____ those who are less fortunate than they.

11. We were short _____ canned food, so we stopped on the way to buy some.

12. The teacher told us _____ severely for passing around notes in class.

13. As she grew older, she became more and more hard _____ hearing.

14. Peter is leaving for New York today, and we are going to the airport to see him _____ .

15. Most of them were down _____ the flu, and so the meeting was called _____ .

PART 18

請在空格中填入合適的介系詞。

1. His parents had hoped that the army would make a man _____ him, but he was kicked out _____ the army.

2. They always made a point _____ coming as early as possible, but today they were held

_____ by a traffic jam.

3. I felt that she was far _____ pleased to see me again.

4. Do you know who is going to take _____ the regiment now that the captain has retired?

5. They made a resolution to bring _____ some reforms in the mining industry.

6. When I mentioned his name, a change came _____ her, and she turned her face away.

7. They are _____ us in this matter; we can totally rely on their support.

8. He is dating a girl, _____ a view to marriage.

9. How _____ inviting our new neighbors over _____ our place for lunch?

10. One day, he will get into trouble _____ the law.

11. He asked _____ my father and promised to come over one day to see him.

12. The streets were covered _____ water, so we sat _____ the fire and talked about our childhood.

13. The rebels had planned to do away _____ the old government and set up a new one.

14. He started work _____ six _____ the morning and continued right up _____ five _____ the evening.

15. There's a "NO ENTRANCE" sign pinned _____ the door. If you go in _____ permission, you'll get _____ trouble.

PART 19

請選擇合適的介系詞填入空格中。

1. Were you quarreling _____ Jimmy just now? I heard you shouting _____ him. (*with; to; at*)

2. Hurry up! It's already a quarter _____ six. We're supposed to be there _____ six. (*by; to*)

3. She fell _____ her bicycle as she was cycling _____ the hill _____ her house _____ the top. (*up; from; to; at*)

4. The thief jumped _____ the window and ran _____ the garden path _____ the gate. (*on; to; through; down*)

5. There was a lovely dress _____ sale _____ the shop _____ the supermarket. She was tempted to buy it, but she didn't have enough money _____ her _____ that moment. (*near; on; with; at; for*)

6. We saw a cat _____ top _____ the cupboard. It was afraid to come down, so I stood _____ a chair, caught hold _____ it and brought it _____ . (on; down; of; on; in)

7. _____ a few minutes, he was back _____ the torch and the rope. We peered _____ the pit with the help _____ the torch. (down; into; within; of; with)

8. He dived _____ the pond and swam _____ the little girl. Catching hold _____ the girl's head, he started to swim _____ the bank. (toward; into; back; of)

9. He spoke _____ me _____ just a few minutes. He said that he was _____ a hurry since he had an appointment _____ an old friend _____ half an hour. (in; with; to; for)

10. I was listening _____ the news _____ the radio when the lights went out suddenly. I jumped out _____ my chair when I felt something brush _____ me. I was so startled that I screamed _____ fright. (of; on; with; against; to; for)

11. If you come _____ Billy _____ your way _____ town, will you please tell him that I will be waiting _____ him _____ Monday to discuss something _____ him? Tell him that it is _____ great importance. (across; with; for; of; on; to; back)

12. Our car broke down while we were passing _____ the village. The three _____ us managed to push the car _____ the nearest garage _____ repairs. We continued the journey _____ foot and reached our place only _____ midnight. (at; through; on; for; of; to; by)

PART 20

請在空格中填入合適的介系詞。

1. She is really good _____ drawing.

2. My new shirt is quite different _____ yours.

3. They are very disappointed _____ her.

4. She was very disappointed _____ not winning the competition.

5. I am not angry _____ you; I am angry _____ what they said.

6. I am very anxious _____ her; all this extra work is not good _____ her.

7. He is always busy _____ his painting.

8. This place is famous _____ its beautiful scenery, and we are all proud _____ it.

9. She has been ill _____ a bad cold and certainly is not fit _____ work.

10. I was shocked _____ the way he had behaved. I hope he is ashamed _____ himself.

11. He was pleased _____ the toy airplane I gave him since he is interested _____ flying.

12. They are very keen _____ this type of work and never get tired _____ doing it.

13. His wife is worried _____ his health. She thinks that all these cigarettes are bad _____ him.

14. It certainly was clever _____ you to have done that. You can be quite certain _____ winning.

PART 21

請在空格中填入合適的介系詞。

1. She frowns _____ those people who gossip _____ their neighbors and friends.

2. The beggar almost fainted _____ hunger, so she hurried _____ the house to get him some food.

3. They apologized _____ their mistake and asked _____ our help to remedy the situation.

4. The dog ran _____ the thief, but he escaped _____ the wall.

5. I have already explained _____ you the qualities of the two articles. You will have to choose _____ them.

6. He ran _____ the corner and hid _____ some garbage cans.

7. They elaborated _____ the subject and explained its importance _____ us.

8. This type of fish feeds _____ insects only and swims rather near the surface _____ the water.

9. While I was collecting donations _____ the blind, I came _____ a friend.

10. The soldier fought _____ anyone who had enough money to pay _____ his services.

11. I managed to inform him _____ the death of his father.

12. The surgeon operated _____ him and removed a cancerous growth _____ his stomach.

13. We had been searching _____ her for almost three hours when we heard her calling _____ help.

14. They were talking _____ the new teacher when I rushed _____ the room.

15. She put the food _____ the table and covered it all _____ a piece of cloth so that the flies could not get _____ anything.

PART 22

請在空格中填入合適的介系詞。

1. Do you happen to know the reason _____ his dismissal _____ the firm?

2. There was an exhibition _____ paintings and sculpture recently.

3. She has a talent _____ making people feel _____ ease with her.

4. Mr. Jones enjoyed great satisfaction _____ the news of his son's success.

5. There is a very marked resemblance _____ the two boys.

6. There is plenty of food _____ everyone present here.

7. They took advantage _____ the fact that the house was empty and lived in it.

8. The new teacher had absolutely no control _____ the class.

9. You have behaved badly and are a disgrace _____ your family.

10. They were holding a discussion _____ the subject of industrialization.

11. She has a great interest _____ science.

12. Many people had shares _____ that company.

13. There was a great response _____ the audience when he appeared on the stage as he had a reputation _____ being witty.

PART 23

請選擇合適的介系詞填入空格中。

1. They will have reached the place _____ tomorrow afternoon. (*on; at; by; after*)

2. It is good to have trees planted _____ the roadsides for shade. (*between; across; along; on*)

3. Have you looked _____ the notes I gave you? (*through; after; on; with*)

4. He tore _____ a sheet of paper from the notebook. (*down; from; off; of*)

5. The village was situated _____ the two hills. (*across; along; under; between*)

6. She has been absent from school _____ Monday. (*for; since; after; on*)

7. The old woman climbed _____ the stairs slowly. (*on; over; above; up*)

8. This machine can be worked _____ electricity only. (*by; on; with; in*)

9. I am leaving _____ Easter Land tomorrow night. (*to; for; at; across*)

10. He was just _____ time for the meeting. (*by; within; in; to*)

11. You really need to work harder. All your marks are _____ average. (*over; above; on; below*)

12. We are usually free _____ six in the evenings. (*on; over; after; for*)

13. I was surprised because for once she had arrived _____ time. (*with; on; at; for*)

14. He cannot be allowed to do this until he is _____ age. (*at; of; under; by*)

15. Is that the lady you were telling me _____? (*of; for; about; with*)

16. What is she complaining _____ now? (*of; in; on; to*)

17. What did she take your book _____? (*for; with; by; about*)

18. All those who are _____ the required age are not allowed in. (*in; below; by*)

PART 24

請在空格中填入合適的介系詞。

1. You will be provided _____ lodging and transportation if you agree _____ my proposal.

2. The doctor advised him to abstain _____ alcoholic drinks and to look _____ his health.

3. He picked _____ the telephone receiver and inserted a quarter _____ the slot.

4. She tidied _____ the bedrooms and prepared _____ the coming of her cousins.

5. They sent her _____ the seaside _____ a week when she had recovered _____ her illness.

6. Why did they call _____ the football match _____ almost the last moment?

7. She took a glance _____ all the letters which were piled _____ the table, but she didn't read them.

8. They always seem to disagree _____ each other _____ the smallest matters.

9. The teacher obtained permission _____ the principal to hold a concert _____ the school hall.

10. I complimented her _____ her good taste _____ decorating the house so skillfully.

11. She trembled _____ the sight of the gun pointed _____ her.

12. The prisoner was sentenced _____ hard labor _____ the rest _____ his life.

13. She was finally persuaded _____ buying the vacuum cleaner _____ the smart salesman.

Chapter 7 | 形容詞

7-1 形容詞的構成

形容詞通常是在動詞或名詞後面加上適當的字尾而構成,常見的字尾有 al、able、ible、ant、ent、y、ic 等,此外還有一些其他的方式可以構成形容詞。

(a) 字尾是 al 或 ial 的形容詞。

USAGE PRACTICE

nature 自然 → natur**al** 自然的

occasion 場合 → occasion**al** 特殊場合的

accident 意外 → accident**al** 意外的

center 中心 → centr**al** 中心的

substance 重要性 → substant**ial** 重要的

commerce 商業 → commerc**ial** 商業的

industry 工業 → industr**ial** 工業的

part 部分 → part**ial** 部分的

continue 繼續 → continu**al** 連續的

person 人 → person**al** 個人的

music 音樂 → music**al** 音樂的

navy 海軍 → nav**al** 海軍的

remedy 治療 → remed**ial** 治療的

ceremony 儀式 → ceremon**ial** 儀式的

colony 殖民地 → colon**ial** 殖民地的

essence 要素 → essent**ial** 要素的

(b) 字尾是 ant 或 ent 的形容詞。

USAGE PRACTICE

distance 距離 → dist**ant** 遠的

ignorance 無知 → ignor**ant** 無知的

abundance 豐富 → abund**ant** 豐富的

defiance 蔑視 → defi**ant** 蔑視的

reliance 依賴 → reli**ant** 依賴的

radiance 發光 → radi**ant** 光芒四射的

patience 耐心 → pati**ent** 有耐心的

presence 出席 → pres**ent** 出席的

excellence 傑出 → excell**ent** 傑出的

difference 不同 → differ**ent** 不同的

triumph 勝利 → triumph**ant** 勝利的

importance 重要 → import**ant** 重要的

fragrance 芳香 → fragr**ant** 芳香的

hesitate 猶豫 → hesit**ant** 猶豫不決的

brilliance 光輝 → brilli**ant** 光輝的

silence 沉默 → sil**ent** 沉默的

absence 缺席 → abs**ent** 缺席的

efficiency 效率 → effici**ent** 有效率的

leniency 寬大 → leni**ent** 寬大的

translucence 半透明 → transluc**ent** 半透明的	transparency 透明 → transpar**ent** 透明的
obedience 服從 → obedi**ent** 服從的	convenience 方便 → conveni**ent** 方便的

(c) 字尾是 able 或 ible 的形容詞。

USAGE PRACTICE

reason 理由 → reason**able** 合理的	advise 勸告 → advis**able** 可取的
break 破碎 → break**able** 會破的	like 喜愛 → like**able** 可愛的
enjoy 得到樂趣 → enjoy**able** 有樂趣的	laugh 笑 → laugh**able** 可笑的
misery 不幸 → miser**able** 不幸的	
terror 驚恐 → terr**ible** 驚恐的	horror 恐怖 → horr**ible** 恐怖的
sense 意識 → sens**ible** 意識到的	force 強迫 → forc**ible** 強迫的
vision 視覺 → vis**ible** 可看見的	

(d) 字尾是 y 或 ly 的形容詞。

USAGE PRACTICE

anger 生氣 → angr**y** 生氣的	rust 鏽 → rust**y** 生鏽的
filth 骯髒 → filth**y** 骯髒的	cloud 雲 → cloud**y** 多雲的
wind 風 → wind**y** 風大的	taste 味道 → tast**y** 美味的
stone 石頭 → ston**y** 石頭的	rock 岩石 → rock**y** 岩石的
hand 手 → hand**y** 手巧的	air 空氣 → air**y** 空氣的
wealth 財富 → wealth**y** 富有的	shade 蔭 → shad**y** 成蔭的
wave 波浪 → wav**y** 波浪的	
day 一天 → dai**ly** 每天的	man 男子 → man**ly** 有男子氣概的
friend 朋友 → friend**ly** 友好的	

(e) 字尾是 ous 或 ious 的形容詞。

USAGE PRACTICE

fame 名聲 → fam**ous** 有名的	poison 毒物 → poison**ous** 有毒的
danger 危險 → danger**ous** 危險的	courage 勇氣 → courage**ous** 有勇氣的

number 數字 → numer**ous** 為數眾多的	monster 怪物 → monstr**ous** 怪物般的
mountain 山 → mountain**ous** 多山的	wonder 驚異 → wondr**ous** 令人驚奇的
joy 高興 → joy**ous** 令人高興的	moment 時刻 → moment**ous** 重要的
victory 勝利 → victor**ious** 勝利的	industry 勤勉 → industr**ious** 勤勉的
envy 嫉妒 → env**ious** 嫉妒的	mystery 神秘 → myster**ious** 神秘的
ambition 野心 → ambit**ious** 有野心的	grace 高雅 → grac**ious** 高雅的
caution 謹慎 → caut**ious** 謹慎的	space 空間 → spac**ious** 廣闊的
anxiety 焦慮 → anx**ious** 焦慮的	fury 狂怒 → fur**ious** 狂怒的

(f) 字尾是 ate 的形容詞。

USAGE PRACTICE

affection 情愛 → affection**ate** 深情的	prime 最好的部分 → prim**ate** 首要的
fortune 運氣 → fortun**ate** 幸運的	moderation 適度 → mode**rate** 適度的
literacy 讀寫的能力 → liter**ate** 有讀寫能力的	passion 熱情 → passion**ate** 熱情的

(g) 字尾是 ary 的形容詞。

USAGE PRACTICE

element 要素 → element**ary** 基本的	honor 名譽 → honor**ary** 名譽上的
station 靜止狀態 → station**ary** 靜止不動的	imagine 想像 → imagin**ary** 想像中的
solitude 孤獨 → solit**ary** 孤獨的	custom 習俗 → custom**ary** 合乎習俗的
second 第二 → second**ary** 第二的	

(h) 字尾是 some 的形容詞。

USAGE PRACTICE

fear 害怕 → fear**some** 可怕的	awe 敬畏 → awe**some** 令人敬畏的
trouble 麻煩 → trouble**some** 麻煩的	quarrel 爭吵 → quarrel**some** 愛爭吵的
tire 使疲倦 → tire**some** 令人疲倦的	meddle 管閒事 → meddle**some** 愛管閒事的
loathe 厭惡 → loath**some** 令人厭惡的	

(i) 字尾是 like 的形容詞。

child 小孩 → child**like** 孩子般的	lady 貴婦 → lady**like** 貴婦般的
life 生命 → life**like** 栩栩如生的	flower 花 → flower**like** 像花一般的

(j) 字尾是 ish 的形容詞。

fool 傻子 → fool**ish** 愚蠢的	book 書本 → book**ish** 喜歡讀書的
sheep 綿羊 → sheep**ish** 膽怯的	snob 自大傲慢的人 → snobb**ish** 自大傲慢的
clown 小丑 → clown**ish** 滑稽的	pink 粉紅色 → pink**ish** 帶粉紅色的
child 小孩子 → child**ish** 幼稚的	self 私心 → self**ish** 自私的
girl 女孩子 → girl**ish** 女孩子氣的	boy 男孩子 → boy**ish** 男孩似的
imp 頑童 → imp**ish** 頑皮的	

(k) 字尾是 ing 的現在分詞可視為形容詞，指「正在發生的事」，也可用來描述「某事
對人的影響」，含有「主動」和「進行」之意。

smile 微笑 → smil**ing** 微笑的	disturb 打擾 → disturb**ing** 擾人的
annoy 使煩惱 → annoy**ing** 令人煩惱的	amuse 使發笑 → amus**ing** 令人發笑的
tire 使疲倦 → tir**ing** 令人疲倦的	surprise 使驚訝 → surpris**ing** 令人驚訝的
excite 使興奮 → excit**ing** 令人興奮的	satisfy 使滿意 → satisfy**ing** 令人滿意的
bore 使厭倦 → bor**ing** 令人厭倦的	interest 使感興趣 → interest**ing** 有趣的
a **smiling** stranger 微笑的陌生人	an **annoying** child 令人討厭的小孩
an **exciting** game 刺激的遊戲	an **interesting** film 有趣的影片
a **satisfying** issue 令人滿意的議題	an **irritating** boy 令人惱怒的男孩
a **laughing** matter 令人發笑的事情	a **giggling** girl 咯咯笑的女孩
the **darkening** sky 正在逐漸變黑的天空	

▶ He had a **tiring** journey. 他進行了一趟累人的旅行。

▶ This is no **laughing** matter. 此事非兒戲。

▶ She put the eggs into the **boiling** water. 她把蛋放進滾水裡。

(l) 字尾是 ed 或 en 的過去分詞可視為形容詞，表示「已發生於某人或某物」，且有「被動」之意。

interest 使感興趣 → interested 感興趣的	boil 煮沸 → boiled 已煮沸的
carve 雕刻 → carved 被雕刻的	paint 油漆 → painted 已上漆的
want 要 → wanted 被通緝的	dry 弄乾 → dried 乾燥的
excite 使興奮 → excited 感到興奮的	amuse 使愉快 → amused 歡樂的
satisfy 使滿意 → satisfied 感到滿意的	annoy 使氣惱 → annoyed 感到氣惱的
rot 腐壞 → rotten 腐壞的	beat 擊敗 → beaten 被擊敗的
an interested buyer 感興趣的買家	a damaged building 被損毀的建築物
an excited boy 感到興奮的男孩	a neglected child 被忽略的孩子
the amused children 被逗樂的孩子們	an unwanted child 多餘的小孩
a wounded soldier 受傷的軍人	a finished project 已經完成的計畫
a pampered girl 被寵壞的女孩	the completed exercise 已經完成的練習
a battered bag 被打扁的袋子	a bored spectator 感到無聊的觀眾

(m) 字尾是 an 或 en 的形容詞。

Hawaii 夏威夷 → Hawaiian 夏威夷的	Italy 義大利 → Italian 義大利的
Chile 智利 → Chilean 智利的	
wood 木頭 → wooden 木製的	gold 金 → golden 金的
wool 羊毛 → woolen 羊毛製的	lead 鉛 → leaden 鉛製的

(n) 字尾是 ive 的形容詞。

mass 大量 → massive 大量的	prevent 預防 → preventive 預防的
decide 決定 → decisive 決定性的	attract 吸引 → attractive 吸引人的
expense 花費 → expensive 昂貴的	act 活動 → active 在活動中的
extend 擴展 → extensive 廣闊的	effect 效果 − effective 有效的

基礎文法寶典 ❷
Essential English Usage & Grammar

erode 侵蝕 → erosive 侵蝕性的   product 產品 → productive 多產的

offense 冒犯 → offensive 冒犯的

(o) 字尾是 ative 的形容詞。

talk 說話 → talkative 喜歡說話的   imagine 想像 → imaginative 有想像力的

(p) 字尾是 ual 的形容詞。

event 事件 → eventual 最終的   sense 感官 → sensual 官能的

continue 繼續 → continual 連續的   habit 習慣 → habitual 習慣性的

spirit 精神 → spiritual 精神（上）的

(q) 字尾是 ful 或 less 的形容詞。

beauty 美麗 → beautiful 美麗的   sorrow 悲傷 → sorrowful 悲傷的

awe 敬畏 → awful 令人敬畏的   heart 愛 → heartless 無情的

star 星 → starless 沒有星光的   home 家 → homeless 無家可歸的

law 法律 → lawful/lawless 合法的／非法的

tear 眼淚 → tearful/tearless 哭泣的／不流淚的

care 小心 → careful/careless 小心的／不小心的

pity 同情 → pitiful/pitiless 令人同情的／無同情心的

pain 疼痛 → painful/painless 疼痛的／不痛的

rest 休息 → restful/restless 給人充分休息的／不休息的

shame 羞恥 → shameful/shameless 可恥的／無恥的

fear 害怕 → fearful/fearless 可怕的／不怕的

(r) 字尾是 ic 的形容詞。

volcano 火山 → volcan**ic** 火山的	hero 英雄 → hero**ic** 英雄的
artist 藝術家 → artist**ic** 藝術的	fantast 幻想家 → fantast**ic** 幻想的
acid 酸 → acid**ic** 酸性的	atom 原子 → atom**ic** 原子的

(s) 字尾是 ar 的形容詞。

USAGE PRACTICE

circle 圓形 → circul**ar** 圓形的	rectangle 長方形 → rectangul**ar** 長方形的
triangle 三角形 → triangul**ar** 三角形的	muscle 肌肉 → muscul**ar** 肌肉發達的

(t) 另外有些形容詞並非由特定字尾構成。

USAGE PRACTICE

old 老的	dry 乾的	open 開放的	warm 溫暖的
young 年輕的	moist 潮濕的	narrow 狹窄的	bitter 苦的
proud 驕傲的	rich 富有的	broad 寬廣的	sweet 甜的

(u) 許多形容詞加上適當的字首就可以構成反義字。

USAGE PRACTICE

un-	**un**exciting 不刺激的 **un**important 不重要的 **un**natural 不自然的 **un**beaten 未被擊敗的	**un**accustomed 不習慣的 **un**common 不尋常的 **un**reliable 不可靠的 **un**armed 未武裝的	**un**conscious 不省人事的 **un**certain 不確定的 **un**tidy 不整潔的 **un**aware 未察覺的
im-	**im**possible 不可能的 **im**probable 不大可能的 **im**moral 不道德的	**im**perfect 不完美的 **im**patient 沒耐心的	**im**personal 沒有人情味的 **im**mature 未成熟的
in-	**in**visible 看不見的 **in**active 不活躍的 **in**animate 無生命的 **in**sensitive 感覺遲鈍的	**in**discreet 不慎重的 **in**complete 不完整的 **in**attentive 不注意的 **in**sincere 不真誠的	**in**curable 無法醫治的 **in**definite 不明確的 **in**capable 不能勝任的
il-	**il**legible 難讀的	**il**logical 不合邏輯的	**il**liberal 不開明的

	illegal 不合法的	**il**literate 不識字的	**il**legitimate 不合法的
ir-	**ir**regular 不規則的	**ir**religious 無宗教的	
dis-	**dis**agreeable 不愉快的	**dis**approving 不贊成的	**dis**pleased 不開心的
	disobedient 不服從的	**dis**respectful 不敬重的	**dis**honest 不誠實的
	distasteful 使人不愉快的	**dis**pleasing 令人不舒服的	
mis-	**mis**guided 被錯誤指導的	**mis**shapen 畸形的	**mis**used 誤用的

小練習

請寫出下列字彙的形容詞形式。

1. hospitality _____   2. reluctance _____   3. include _____

4. ritual _____   5. fancy _____   6. leniency _____

7. irritate _____   8. hate _____   9. legibility _____

10. doubt _____   11. impulse _____   12. wrath _____

13. wealth _____   14. expense _____   15. resource _____

16. stimulate _____   17. nation _____   18. experience _____

19. remove _____   20. origin _____   21. criticize _____

22. disobedience _____   23. risk _____   24. significance _____

☞ 更多相關習題請見本章應用練習 Part 1～Part 8。

7-2 形容詞的種類

(a) 形容詞用於修飾名詞，可分為六大類。

性狀形容詞	good 好的	stupid 愚笨的	clever 聰明的
	excellent 傑出的	bold 大膽的	ugly 醜的
	high 高的	noble 高貴的	funny 有趣的
數量形容詞	many 許多的	much 許多的	plenty 許多的
	three 三個的	thousand 一千的	dozen 一打的
	first 第一的		
所有形容詞	my 我的	your 你的	his 他的
	her 她的	its 它／牠的	our 我們的

	their 他們的		
指示形容詞	this 這 those 那些	that 那 neither 兩者都不	these 這些 either 兩者之中任一的
不定形容詞	each 每一個 some 一些	every 每一個 one 某一個的	any 任何
疑問形容詞	whose 誰的	which 哪一個	what 什麼

7-3 所有形容詞

(a) 所有形容詞就是人稱代名詞的所有格，表示「所有權」。而所有格代名詞則可以取代「所有形容詞＋名詞」。

USAGE PRACTICE

所有形容詞 + 名詞	所有格代名詞
▶ This is **my** pen. 這是我的筆。	→ This pen is **mine.** 這筆是我的。
▶ It is **my** bag. 它是我的袋子	→ It is **mine.** 它是我的。
▶ That is **our** car. 那是我們的汽車。	→ That car is **ours.** 那部汽車是我們的。
▶ Where are **our** seats? 我們的座位在哪裡？	→ Where are **ours**? 我們的在哪裡？
▶ Is this **your** cat? 這是你的貓嗎？	→ Is this cat **yours**? 這貓是你的嗎？
▶ This is **your** purse. 這是你的皮包。	→ This is **yours**. 這是你的。
▶ He has done **his** work. 他已經完成他的工作。	→ He has done **his**. 他已經完成他的了。
▶ This is **his** house. 這是他的房子。	→ This is **his**. 這是他的。
▶ Are these **her** glasses? 這是她的眼鏡嗎？	→ Are these glasses **hers**? 這眼鏡是她的嗎？
▶ That is **her** book. 那是她的書。	→ That is **hers**. 那是她的。
▶ Are you **their** friend? 你是他們的朋友嗎？	→ Are you a friend of **theirs**? 你是他們的一個朋友嗎？
▶ Let's borrow **their** books.	→ Let's borrow **theirs**. 我們來借他們的吧。

基礎文法寶典 ❷
Essential English Usage & Grammar

我們來借他們的書吧。

▶ The hen sat on **its** eggs.

母雞在孵它的蛋。

▶ This is **its** tail. 這是它的尾巴。

（its 這個所有格代名詞很少使用。）

 注意 請特別注意名詞所有格、所有形容詞與所有格代名詞的區別。

▶ This is the **boy's** watch. 這是這男孩的手錶。（名詞所有格）
→ This is **his** watch. 這是他的手錶。（所有形容詞）
→ This watch is **his**. 這手錶是他的。（所有格代名詞）
▶ This is the **lady's** bag. 這是這女士的手袋。（名詞所有格）
→ This is **her** bag. 這是她的手袋。（所有形容詞）
→ This bag is **hers**. 這手袋是她的。（所有格代名詞）

(b) 所有形容詞後面通常必須接一個名詞，而所有格代名詞則可以單獨使用。

USAGE PRACTICE

▶ I have taken **my** book. 我已經拿了我的書。

▶ This is **my** dress. 這是我的洋裝。

▶ Are these **your** handkerchiefs? 這些是你的手帕嗎？

▶ This is **your** shirt and that is **his** shirt. 這是你的襯衫，那是他的襯衫。

▶ **His** father has signed **his** report card. 他爸爸已經簽了他的成績單。

▶ I think **her** friends are getting impatient. 我想她的朋友們漸漸不耐煩了。

▶ Hold the dog by **its** collar. 抓住那隻狗的項圈。

▶ I didn't bring **my** book. Can I share **yours**（所有格代名詞）?

　我沒帶我的書來，我能和你共用你的嗎？

▶ Which of these is **mine**（所有格代名詞）? 這些當中的那一個是我的？

▶ I took **her** book; she took **yours**（所有格代名詞）. 我拿了她的書；她拿了你的。

▶ I am worried about **my** own problems; I have no time to worry about **his**（所有格代名詞）.

　我擔心自己的問題，沒有時間去擔心他的。

▶ Those shoes are not **ours**（所有格代名詞）but **theirs**（所有格代名詞）.

　那些鞋子不是我們的而是他們的。

不可把 its 和 it's 混淆,前者是 it 的所有形容詞,而後者是 it is 的縮寫。

▶ That is **its** bone. 那是牠的骨頭。

▶ The cat is licking **its** face. 這隻貓正在舔牠的臉。

▶ The tiger has eaten **its** dinner. 這隻老虎已經吃完牠的晚餐了。

▶ The dog wagged **its** tail at the sight of **its** master. 這隻狗一看到牠的主人就搖尾巴。

▶ **It's** a bottle of milk. 它是一瓶牛奶。(It's = It is)

(c) 所有形容詞必須與主詞的格和數一致。

USAGE PRACTICE

▶ I have lost **my** bag. 我遺失了我的袋子。

▶ The little girl is tugging at **her** mother's skirt. 小女孩拉著她媽媽的裙子。

▶ The boys wanted **their** ball back. 這些男孩們想要回他們的球。

▶ We had **our** dinner early. 我們很早吃了晚餐。

▶ Mr. Richards nearly tripped over **his** shoelace. 理查先生差點被他的鞋帶絆倒。

▶ Are you out of **your** mind? 你瘋了嗎?

小練習

請填入正確的所有形容詞或所有格代名詞。

1. I think she can do it on _____ own.

2. The boys are shouting at the top of _____ voices.

3. I'll have _____ breakfast and go over to John's house.

4. "Are these your books?" "No, these certainly are not _____ books. John, are they _____?"

5. We have not made up _____ minds yet, but they seem to have made up _____ already.

6. He asked some friends of _____ to come over to _____ house for a chat.

7. Haven't you finished _____ work yet? I have already finished _____.

8. Give it back to me. It's not _____; it's _____.

9. The dog wagged _____ tail when it saw _____ master approaching.

10. I think _____ work is much better done than _____ since they got lower scores than we did.

11. Did anyone see Sally's bag anywhere? _____ bag is missing.

12. I must thank him for lending me _____ books. They helped me a lot in _____ work.

13. David and Lily were taking _____ dog for a walk when it broke _____ leash and dashed off on _____ own.

14. We often do _____ homework together. She checks _____ work, and I check _____ .

15. Has _____ sister lost _____ mind, Peter? And have you lost _____ too?

☞ 更多相關習題請見本章應用練習 Part 9～Part 12。

7-4 不定形容詞 some、any 及其他

(a) 當數量不明確時，some 和 any 可以修飾可數和不可數名詞。

USAGE PRACTICE
▶ There are **some** pickled mangoes. 有一些醃芒果。
▶ She is buying **some** flour. 她正在買一些麵粉。
▶ There is **some** milk in the jug. 壺裡有一些牛奶。
▶ **Some** boys are playing football on the field. 一些男孩正在球場玩美式足球。
▶ Are there **any** books on the shelf? 架子上有任何書嗎？
▶ There isn't **any** flour left in the bowl. 碗裡沒有任何麵粉剩下來。

(b) some 通常用於肯定句。

USAGE PRACTICE
▶ She poured **some** oil into the frying pan. 她把一些油倒進煎鍋裡。
▶ She offered me **some** advice. 她給我一些忠告。
▶ I put **some** sugar in my tea. 我放一些糖在茶裡。
▶ There is **some** coffee left in the pot. 壺裡還剩下一些咖啡。
▶ The pail contains **some** water. 桶子裡有一些水。
▶ He met **some** friends at the movie theater last night. 昨晚他在電影院遇到一些朋友。
▶ The teacher took away **some** books from the boys. 老師拿走這些男孩的一些書。
▶ There are **some** cookies here. I'll have **some** even though you don't want any.

這裡有一些餅乾。即使你都不要，我還是會吃一些。

▶ I will need **some** money if I am to go there. 如果要去那裡，我會需要一些錢。

▶ I have **some** ointment here that might be good for you.

我這裡有一些可能對你有幫助的藥膏。

 但是，當說話者期望肯定的回答，或當說話者給予請求或提議時，some 可以用在疑問句。

▶ Aren't there **some** books that I can read? 沒有一些我可以讀的書嗎？（期望肯定的回答）

▶ Are there **some** stamps in the drawer? 抽屜裡有一些郵票嗎？（期望肯定的回答）

▶ Didn't I give you **some** money earlier? 之前我不是給過你一些錢嗎？（期望肯定的回答）

▶ Is there still **some** coffee left? 還有剩下一些咖啡嗎？（期望肯定的回答）

▶ Will you please boil **some** water? 可以請你煮一些水嗎？（表示請求）

▶ Can I have **some** more sugar in my coffee, please? 我的咖啡可以再加一些糖嗎？（表示請求）

▶ Won't you have **some** more cookies? 你不再多吃一些餅乾嗎？（表示提議）

(c) any 則多用在否定句和疑問句。

USAGE PRACTICE

▶ I don't want **any** coffee. 我不想要任何咖啡。

▶ He did not offer **any** advice to her. 他沒有給她任何忠告。

▶ The teacher did not take away **any** books from the boys.

老師並沒有拿走這些男孩的任何書本。

▶ He did not meet **any** friends at the movie theater last night.

昨晚他在電影院沒有遇見任何朋友。

▶ She hasn't had **any** food to eat for more than a day.

她已經超過一天沒有任何食物可吃了。

▶ Is there **any** salt left in the bowl? 碗裡還有剩下任何鹽嗎？

▶ Is there **any** food on the table? 桌上有任何食物嗎？

▶ Did she offer you **any** advice? 她給了你任何忠告嗎？

▶ Can you find **any** mistakes in the essay? 你可以在這篇文章中找到任何錯誤嗎？

▶ Have you got **any** coins to make a phone call? 你有硬幣可以打電話嗎？

(d) 在單數名詞前可以使用 some 來表示「某個」。

USAGE PRACTICE

▶ I must have come across this word in **some** book. 我一定在某本書看過這個字。

▶ He gave me **some** idea of what to do. 他給我某個該如何做的意見。

▶ Can't you give me **some** idea of what to expect? 你不能給我某個該期待什麼的意見嗎？

▶ He went to **some** place in India last year. 去年他去印度的某個地方。

(e) 複數可數名詞還可以用 a few、many、a lot of、a large number of 等不定形容詞來修飾，且與複數動詞連用。

USAGE PRACTICE

▶ **A few** boys have volunteered to help. 有些男孩已經自願幫忙。

▶ There were **a large number of** guests at the party. 宴會裡有很多客人。

▶ **Many** hands make light work. 人手多工作就輕鬆。

▶ **A lot of** children like these toys. 很多小孩子喜歡這些玩具。

請在空格中填入合適的不定形容詞（或不定代名詞）some 或 any。

1. He doesn't want _____ cakes, but he would like to have _____ lemonade.

2. She asked me for _____ magazines, but I could not find _____ .

3. The girls didn't bring _____ towels with them, so I lent them _____ of mine.

4. We don't have _____ time now, but we will drop by when we have _____ time.

5. Help yourself to _____ of these cookies. You may have _____ of those candies, too.

6. Do you have _____ coins with you? I need _____ to put in the parking meter.

7. Could you go to the shop to buy me _____ bread? There isn't _____ left in the house.

8. Didn't you meet _____ of your friends at the party last night? I was sure _____ of them were there.

9. How could _____ of us know where you had gone when you did not leave _____ word behind?

10. _____ of you may know about it because _____ of your friends may have been there when it occurred.

11. _____ of my stationery is missing from the drawer. Do _____ of you know where it might have gone?

12. I do not have _____ stamps of this kind in my collection, but I do have _____ of that type.

13. Did you see _____ hawkers selling eggs at the market while you were there? I need _____ to make the cake.

☞ 更多相關習題請見本章應用練習 Part 13～Part 16。

7-5 形容詞的用法、位置與順序

(a) 形容詞通常置於其所修飾的名詞之前。

USAGE PRACTICE

▶ The **guilty** party accepted the punishment quietly. 有罪的一方安靜地接受處罰。

▶ He was a **model** student in school. 他在學校是模範生。

▶ She gave him an **angry** look. 她生氣地看他一眼。

▶ The **angry** father punished the **naughty** child. 這生氣的父親處罰他頑皮的小孩。

▶ The **tired** worker was glad to have a **cold** drink. 這個疲勞的工人很高興能喝一杯冷飲。

▶ The **pretty** girl walked slowly down the **crowded** street.

　這漂亮的女孩慢慢地沿著擁擠的街道走著。

▶ We cannot afford to buy **expensive** shoes. 我們買不起昂貴的鞋子。

(b) 形容詞置於主詞與 be 動詞之後。

USAGE PRACTICE

▶ His voice is **loud** and **clear**. 他的聲音大而清楚。

▶ The dress was **pretty** but **expensive**. 這衣裳很漂亮但很貴。

▶ The day was **windy**. 那天颳著風。

▶ They were **exhausted** after their long walk. 在走了很長的路之後，他們筋疲力盡。

▶ She was **missing**, so I went to look for her. 她失蹤了，所以我去找她。

▶ The girl was **happy** when she received the letter. 當這個女孩接到這封信時，她很高興。

▶ He was **quick-tempered** but **kind**. 他脾氣急躁但很仁慈。

> The door is **shut** but the windows are **open**. 這扇門是緊閉的，但是窗戶是開的。

(c) 形容詞置於主詞與連綴動詞 look、seem、appear、become、feel 等之後。

USAGE PRACTICE

▶ He looked very **pale** when he came out of the hospital. 當他從醫院出來時，臉色非常蒼白。

▶ That girl looks **lovely** in that skirt. 那個女孩穿那件裙子看起來很可愛。

▶ That woman seems **angry** with you. 那個婦人好像在生你的氣。

▶ He appeared **angry** when she scolded him. 當她罵他的時候，他看起來很生氣。

▶ She became **rich** after inheriting her uncle's property.
在繼承她叔叔的財產後，她變得富有。

▶ The climb became more **difficult** later on. 後來，攀登變得更困難了。

▶ He felt **tired** and **depressed**. 他覺得疲憊又沮喪。

(d) 許多形容詞和介系詞可以構成慣用語。

USAGE PRACTICE

▶ He is **famous** for his generosity to orphans. 他因為對孤兒慷慨而出名。

▶ I was **surprised** at the value of those paintings. 我對那些畫的價值感到驚訝。

▶ It was fortunate that he was **honest** with you. 很幸運地，他對你很誠實。

▶ Bullies are usually **afraid** of the slightest danger. 惡人沒膽。

▶ He is very **proud** of his achievements. 他為自己的成就感到十分驕傲。

▶ He is very **fond** of reading detective novels. 他非常喜歡閱讀偵探小說。

▶ I will be **frank** with you. 我會對你坦白。

▶ She was **anxious** for my safety. 她擔心我的安全。

▶ She was **shocked** at the way they talked. 她對他們講話的方式感到震驚。

▶ He was **angry** at being disturbed. 他因被打擾而生氣。

▶ This design is **different** from hers. 這個設計和她的不同。

(e) 當兩個或兩個以上的形容詞連用時，要注意其順序。以下的表格為常用的形容詞
排序，但並非固定規則；如果要強調某個特質時，可以改變順序。

限定詞	性質	大小、形狀	顏色	材質	執行、動力	名詞
a few 幾個	sour 酸的		green 綠色的			mangoes 芒果
a 一個		high 高的	gray 灰色的	stone 石頭的		wall 牆
many 許多	pretty 漂亮的		blue 藍色的	silk 絲質的		gown 禮服
an 一個	useful 有用的	long 長的	black 黑色的	leather 皮的		cases 盒子
the second 第二		big square 大的方形	black 黑色的	steel 鋼製的	steam 蒸汽的	engine 引擎
a few 一些	new 新的	circular 圓的		metal 金屬的	automatic 自動的	clocks 時鐘
this 這個	strong 堅硬的	large 大的	red 紅色的			ring 環
some 一些	clean 乾淨的	square 方形的	white 白色的	linen 亞麻的		sheets 被單
the 這	old 老舊的				mechanical 機械的	toys 玩具

(f) 按照文法規則，當作形容詞用的名詞要用單數形，但是有些使用複數形。

USAGE PRACTICE

a **pattern** book 一本句型書　　　　a five-**dollar** bill 一張五元鈔票

a ten-**meter** ladder 一把十公尺的梯子　　a **garden** party 一個花園派對

a **games** master 一位體育老師　　　the **plastics** industry 塑膠業

our **sports** meet 我們的學校運動會　　the **Statistics** Department 統計部

(g) 當表示「特性」、「數量」或「測量」等之意時，形容詞可置於名詞或代名詞之後。

基礎文法寶典 ❷
Essential English Usage & Grammar

> **USAGE PRACTICE**
>
> ▶ The building is thirty stories **high**. 那棟大樓有三十層高。
>
> ▶ Do Exercise **Ten** now. 現在做練習十。
>
> ▶ I want a plank twenty-five centimeters **wide** and fifty centimeters **long**.
>
> 我要一塊二十五公分寬、五十公分長的木板。
>
> ▶ That man claimed to be over a hundred years **old**. 那男人聲稱超過一百歲了。

(h) 某些特定形容詞也可以置於名詞之後。

> **USAGE PRACTICE**
>
> time **immemorial** 遠古   the people **present** 在場的人

(i) 也可用連接詞連接兩個形容詞。

> **USAGE PRACTICE**
>
> ▶ The old man, **poor but proud**, refused to beg. 這老人，貧窮但驕傲，拒絕乞討。
>
> ▶ That girl, **pretty and gentle**, is liked by all. 那個女孩，漂亮又溫和，讓所有人都喜歡。

(j) 表示特質的形容詞前面加上定冠詞，可以用來表達名詞的意思，指「該類的人」（複數涵義）。

> **USAGE PRACTICE**
>
> ▶ The **good** will be rewarded and the **bad** punished. 好人有好報，壞人有壞報。
>
> ▶ The **strong** are looked up to by the **meek** and the **mild**.
>
> 個性溫和柔順的人尊敬個性剛強的人。

7-6 形容詞的句型

(a) S + be + Adj + to V...

> **USAGE PRACTICE**
>
> ▶ I will be **glad** to receive the prize on his behalf. 我會很高興代替他領獎。
>
> ▶ We are **glad** to know of your safe arrival. 我們很高興知道你安全到達。

▶ She is very **anxious** to buy it. 她渴望買下它。

▶ He was **disappointed** to hear the news. 他聽到這個消息很失望。

▶ He was **lucky** to win the first prize. 他很幸運能贏得最大獎。

▶ He was **amazed** to see the old man dancing. 他很驚訝看到這老人跳舞。

▶ I am **sorry** to tell you that the airplane has left. 我很遺憾地告訴你這班飛機已經起飛了。

▶ I was **sorry** to hear the tragic news. 我很遺憾聽到這悲慘的消息。

▶ I was **shocked** to hear of his insolent behavior. 聽到他的傲慢行為，我感到震驚。

(b) S + be + too + Adj (+ for sb) + to V...

USAGE PRACTICE

▶ The criminal was too **ashamed** to see his parents. 這罪犯太羞愧而無顏見他的父母。

▶ He is too **young** to start school this year. 他年紀太小今年還不能開始上學。

▶ The thread is too **thick** to go through the needle. 這線太粗無法穿過針孔。

▶ The box is too **heavy** for me to carry. 這個箱子太重了，我搬不動。

▶ The problem was too **difficult** for me to solve. 這問題太難了，我沒辦法解決。

▶ He is too **young** to understand this matter. 他太年輕了，無法了解這件事。

▶ He is too **fat** to crawl under the fence. 他太胖以至於無法從籬笆下爬過去。

▶ They were too **angry** to listen to any reasons. 他們太生氣了，不願意聽任何理由。

(c) S + be + Adj + enough + to V...

USAGE PRACTICE

▶ The water is **hot** enough to boil the eggs. 這水熱得足以把蛋煮熟。

▶ He is **old** enough to look after himself. 他年紀夠大，足以照顧自己了。

▶ He was **foolish** enough to make that mistake. 他犯那個錯實在有夠愚蠢。

▶ She is **small** enough to crawl through that hole. 她身材夠小，足以爬過那個洞。

▶ You are **intelligent** enough to solve this problem. 你夠聰明來解決這個問題。

▶ You are **good** enough to win the championship. 你的實力夠，足以贏得冠軍。

(d) S + be + so + Adj. + that...

基礎文法寶典 ❷
Essential English Usage & Grammar

USAGE PRACTICE

▶ They were so **busy** in the garden that they did not hear the scream.

他們在花園裡是那麼忙碌以至於沒有聽到尖叫的聲音。

▶ She is so **bad-tempered** that no one likes her. 她的脾氣如此差以至於沒有人喜歡她。

▶ The spectators were so **excited** that they cheered without ceasing.

觀眾們如此興奮以至於他們不停地歡呼。

▶ The explosion was so **loud** that it was heard by all the villagers.

爆炸如此大聲以至於全部的村民都聽見了。

▶ I was so **tired** that I fell asleep at once. 我如此累以至於立刻就睡著了。

▶ The lesson was so **boring** that half the students were dozing in their seats.

這課是如此無趣以至於有一半的學生坐在他們的位子上打瞌睡。

▶ The joke was so **funny** that everyone burst out laughing.

這個笑話是如此好笑，所以每個人都突然笑出來。

▶ He was so **stubborn** that he refused to listen to any of us.

他如此地頑固以至於拒絕聽我們任何人的話。

(e) S + be + as + Adj + as...

USAGE PRACTICE

▶ The acrobat was as **agile** as a monkey. 這雜技演員像猴子一樣敏捷。

▶ He is as **old** as my grandfather. 他像我的祖父一樣老。

▶ They are not as **hardworking** as you are. 他們不像你們工作那麼努力。

(f) S + be/V + 比較級 Adj (+ N) + than...

USAGE PRACTICE

▶ She is **cleverer** than I am. 她比我聰明。

▶ Your dress is **prettier** than hers. 你的衣裳比她的漂亮。

▶ You are **more obstinate** than he is. 你比他頑固。

▶ The weather today is **worse** than it was yesterday. 今天的天氣比昨天的糟糕。

▶ I had **lower** marks on the tests than she. 我這次考試得到的分數比她得到的更低。

▶ The pen is **mightier** than the sword. 文勝於武。

(g) S + be + the + 最高級 Adj...

USAGE PRACTICE

This is the **thickest** rope I can find. 這是我能找到最粗的繩子。

That is the **ugliest** of all the goblins. 那是所有妖怪當中最醜陋的一個。

I caught the **biggest** of all the fish that day. 那天我捕獲所有魚中最大的一條。

That is the **most expensive** of all the bags here. 那是這裡所有手提袋中最貴的一個。

She is the **most beautiful** girl I have seen. 她是我見過最美麗的女孩。

She is the **best** student in my class. 她是我班上最好的學生。

That was the **most amazing** feat he had ever performed. 那是他曾經表演過最驚人的技藝。

請利用前面所學過的的句型來合併以下句子。

1. Sally is 17 years old. I'm 17, too.

   → _____

2. It will be easy enough. You can learn on your own.

   → _____

3. I had 10 video games. Matthew had 12 video games.

   → _____

4. The water is warm enough. We can swim.

   → _____

5. The bread was too stale. It could not be eaten.

   → _____

6. Judy is very smart. No one in this class is smarter than she.

   → _____

7. The bag is so large. You can put all these things into it.

   → _____

8. The book is interesting. That book is more interesting.

   → _____

9. This book is too difficult. I don't understand.

→ _____

10. Jerry was so kind. Everyone liked him very much.

→ _____

Chapter 7　應用練習

PART 1

請寫出下列字彙的形容詞形式。

1. fever _____
2. complement _____
3. stone _____
4. humor _____
5. accident _____
6. sensation _____
7. spice _____
8. importance _____
9. history _____
10. comfort _____
11. rely _____
12. divide _____
13. meddle _____
14. sorrow _____
15. rectangle _____
16. piety _____
17. sanitation _____

PART 2

請寫出下列字彙的形容詞形式。

1. fame _____
2. triangle _____
3. snob _____
4. vigor _____
5. hygiene _____
6. danger _____
7. science _____
8. chaos _____
9. boy _____
10. mischief _____
11. attract _____
12. fury _____
13. monster _____
14. acrobat _____
15. habit _____
16. fool _____
17. caution _____
18. insult _____
19. progress _____
20. solitude _____
21. persuade _____
22. produce _____
23. energy _____

PART 3

請寫出下列字彙的形容詞形式。

1. poison _____
2. influence _____
3. sympathy _____
4. coward _____
5. atom _____
6. China _____

7. compliment _____ 8. number _____ 9. honor _____

10. economy _____ 11. study _____ 12. democracy _____

13. space _____ 14. arm _____

PART 4

請寫出下列字彙的形容詞形式。

1. center _____ 2. crime _____ 3. fashion _____

4. type _____ 5. possess _____ 6. obey _____

7. giant _____ 8. mystery _____ 9. excess _____

10. haste _____ 11. person _____ 12. hero _____

13. disaster _____ 14. muscle _____ 15. memory _____

16. envy _____ 17. attend _____ 18. silence _____

19. hunger _____ 20. deceit _____ 21. advise _____

PART 5

請寫出下列形容詞的反義字。

1. logical _____ 2. resolute _____ 3. compatible _____

4. competent _____ 5. real _____ 6. used _____

7. relevant _____ 8. qualified _____ 9. questioned _____

10. pleasing _____ 11. soluble _____ 12. combustible _____

13. satisfied _____ 14. thinkable _____ 15. scrupulous _____

16. tiring _____ 17. passionate _____ 18. similar _____

19. constant _____ 20. removable _____ 21. reputable _____

22. potent _____ 23. practicable _____

PART 6

請選擇正確的形容詞形式填入空格中。

1. The _____ (*drowned, drowning*) boy shouted for help before he was swept away the falls.

2. The old beggar wore _____ (*torn, tearing*) clothes which were patched in a dozen places.

3. After an _____ (*annoyed, annoying*) delay, we finally managed to start on our journey.

4. The _____ (*increased, increasing*) number of diseases in this region is of concern to the

authorities.

5. The _____ (*excited, exciting*) boy jumped up and down when he heard the news.

6. It was a _____ (*bored, boring*) film that was shown at the Grand Cinema yesterday.

7. He had an _____ (*amused, amusing*) smile on his face when he came into the room.

8. We gazed in silence at the _____ (*burned, burning*) village where we had spent all our childhood.

9. It was already _____ (*closed, closing*) time, and the shopkeeper was in a hurry to go home.

10. The campers had _____ (*burned, burning*) rice for supper, but they still enjoyed it.

11. He was too _____ (*absorbed, absorbing*) in watching the game on television to pay attention to her grumbling.

12. I witnessed an _____ (*amused, amusing*) incident while I was passing the _____ (*haunted, haunting*) house on the edge of the village.

13. The _____ (*frightening, frightened*) child cowered in a corner at the sight of the stranger.

PART 7

請選擇正確的形容詞形式填入空格中。

1. **disappointed, disappointing**

   (a) Last year, the results of the examination were rather _____ .

   (b) I am very _____ to know that you can't come to my party.

2. **insulted, insulting**

   (a) He felt _____ that you didn't invite him to the dinner.

   (b) The fight started because of an _____ remark that he had made.

3. **pleased, pleasing**

   (a) They all liked him because he had a _____ personality.

   (b) She seemed _____ to know that I was going with them.

4. **irritated, irritating**

   (a) When he is _____ , he usually starts grumbling about everything.

   (b) The noise that children make can be rather _____ , especially when you are trying to concentrate.

5. **bored, boring**

(a) It was such a _____ film that he fell asleep halfway through it.

(b) You can see that the spectators are _____ when some of them yawn or move around.

6. **puzzled, puzzling**

(a) It was a _____ question and he could find no answer to it.

(b) She was walking past and she had a _____ frown on her face.

7. **exhausted, exhausting**

(a) It was an _____ climb, but the sight from the hilltop was worth the climb.

(b) After running a few hundred meters, they were soon _____ and out of breath.

8. **increased, increasing**

(a) The _____ number of patients at the hospital was alarming.

(b) They were willing to rent out their boats, but only at an _____ rate.

9. **interested, interesting**

(a) You are such an _____ person. I want to get to know you better.

(b) He told the story to an _____ audience of young children.

10. **satisfied, satisfying**

(a) I've just had a _____ meal; now all I want to do is sleep.

(b) Mr. Jones is very _____. He has just completed a big business deal.

11. **amazed, amazing**

(a) The boy was so _____ when he saw Chien-Ming Wang that he didn't know what to do.

(b) He was dumbfounded when he heard the _____ news.

12. **comforted, comforting**

(a) The nurse's touch was so _____ that her patient calmed down at once.

(b) The _____ boy fell asleep almost immediately.

13. **shocked, shocking**

(a) The _____ scandal was published in all the newspapers.

(b) The people were _____ when they read about the scandal.

14. **distinguished, distinguishing**

(a) He was _____ for his works of art.

(b) Those boys are twins, but you can tell who is who by a few _____ moles.

15. **tired, tiring**

(a) I have had a _____ day; I've been cleaning the house the whole morning.

(b) He was so _____ that he could hardly stand.

16. **affected, affecting**

(a) He assumed an _____ politeness when he spoke to his rival.

(b) When he saw the _____ sight, he decided to donate his entire fortune to the charity.

17. **darkened, darkening**

(a) When he saw the _____ sky, he decided to take an umbrella with him.

(b) I couldn't see anything clearly in the _____ room.

18. **fallen, falling**

(a) The elephant dragged the _____ tree down to the river.

(b) When they saw the _____ tree, they ran for their lives.

PART 8

請參考提示字，將正確的形容詞填入空格中。

1. Those people are very _____ (*friend*) to strangers; they are also _____ (*religion*) people.

2. We could not hear his _____ (*stealth*) footsteps as he crept into the house.

3. He is quite an _____ (*innocence*) child. I don't think what he said was _____ (*intention*).

4. That _____ (*India*) woman has a _____ (*remark*) sense of balance. Look at her walking with a jar of water on her head!

5. The _____ (*silver*) surface of the lake was rippling in the breeze and there was a moon above. It was an _____ (*enchant*) night!

6. The garden looked _____ (*neglect*), for weeds had sprung up everywhere.

7. The _____ (*origin*) document was destroyed in a _____ (*rage*) fire two years ago.

8. Betty is generally an _____ (*obey*) child, but today she made a _____ (*deliberation*) attempt to disobey her mother.

9. The trapeze artist performed many acts which were _____ (*sensation*) and extremely _____ (*danger*).

10. The woman developed a _____ (*trouble*) allergy to insecticide and therefore had a _____ (*difficulty*) time finding work on a vegetation farm.

11. Mr. Robinson, who was used to _____ (*Europe*) dishes, could not take the _____ (*spice*) _____ (*Asia*) food.

12. They had _____ (*break*) nails and _____ (*blister*) hands when they had finished digging.

13. The government introduced _____ (*progress*) taxation as a _____ (*fairness*) means of obtaining revenue.

14. What we want is _____ (*construct*) not _____ (*destruct*) criticism.

15. He is _____ (*attract*) and has a _____ (*charm*) personality, too.

16. Don't be _____ (*impatience*) with her; she may be slow but she is _____ (*steadiness*) in her work.

17. The _____ (*follow*) passage is taken from a _____ (*simplify*) version of the book, *Jane Eyre*.

18. The firm is advertising for a _____ (*responsibility*) young man who is _____ (*will*) to undertake some _____ (*exhaust*) but _____ (*reward*) work.

PART 9

請填入正確的所有形容詞或所有格代名詞。

1. Have you finished _____ essay? Most of us have handed in _____ and Andrew has even had _____ corrected.

2. I'm sure that Alex and Jane are at home. Let's go to _____ house. I want to show them _____ new bicycle.

3. Pamela is celebrating _____ eighteenth birthday. Some friends of _____ have come to give her _____ best wishes.

4. _____ mother scolded him for dirtying _____ shirt. She did _____ best but the stain just wouldn't come off.

5. "Have you swept _____ classroom?" "Yes, we have cleaned _____, and _____ teacher praised us for _____ efforts."

6. I have lost _____ pen. It was one of _____ best pens. Have you or any of _____ friends seen it? _____ cap is bright yellow.

7. This lazy man has never done a stroke of work in _____ life. He expects _____ family to support him. A sister of _____ scolded him the other day. _____ words

would have made any man feel ashamed of himself.

8. Lucy and I were taking _____ daily walk when we met a friend. She invited us to go to _____ house to see a rare plant of _____ .

9. It's raining. If you don't have _____ umbrella, you may take _____ . I have to finish _____ work and _____ brother will come later and drive me home.

10. What a beautiful baby this is! _____ face is pink and healthy; it's kicking out with all _____ might. But I think that _____ diaper is wet. I wonder where _____ mother is; it's not safe to leave a baby alone in a baby carriage.

11. A student told me that you had lost _____ racket. Is this _____ ? I found it under a tree in the school garden.

12. I don't think that you have returned _____ book yet. I lent _____ to you when you didn't bring _____ . I need _____ now to help my brother with _____ work.

13. Tom and Henry have not changed _____ minds about buying that factory, but we have changed _____ . We hope that _____ venture will be successful; those plans of _____ are not too sound.

14. Billy has put _____ marbles here. Luckily you do not mix up _____ with _____ ; otherwise both of you will have a hard time sorting out _____ marbles.

15. Susan is driving _____ father's car because _____ is being repaired at the garage. _____ father has told her that she can use _____ as long as she is careful with it.

16. The staff will be having _____ annual dinner next week. Everyone is doing _____ best to help. The women are pouring over _____ recipe books and some of them have promised to cook _____ special dishes.

PART 10

請填入正確的所有形容詞或所有格代名詞。

1. We nearly lost _____ way through the jungle. _____ guide wasn't familiar with that part of it.

2. My cousin came to borrow _____ umbrella because he had left _____ at home.

3. It isn't fair! They have eaten all _____ food and they have come to take _____ . We refuse to give them _____ .

4. _____ parents were away, so we asked her to stay at _____ house for the weekend.

5. All the people clapped _____ hands when the singer made _____ entrance on stage.

6. Jack took out _____ handkerchief to mop _____ brow, but Jill fanned herself with _____ .

7. Your dog and _____ were fighting just now. Look! My dog has hurt _____ paw. It's bleeding.

8. When you have finished _____ work, you may go. Anyone who hasn't finished _____ must stay behind to complete it.

9. The Smiths came in _____ car and we followed behind in _____ .

10. The dog pricked up _____ ears and gave a low growl.

11. The other divers put on _____ diving suits and he did the same with _____ .

12. I have had _____ dinner. Have you had _____ ?

13. Andy gave me _____ address, but Susan didn't give me _____ .

14. "Jane, when you have finished _____ homework, you must help your sister with _____ ," Mother said.

15. _____ cook had to leave right away because _____ mother was ill, so we had to do _____ own cooking for the rest of that month.

16. As Peter was walking along, someone tapped _____ shoulder. Peter turned around and saw _____ old classmate, Jeffrey.

17. Jimmy was looking for _____ book. He couldn't find _____ , so he had to borrow _____ . He wants me to help return it to her now.

18. This puppy has lost _____ mother. We must do _____ best to look after it.

PART 11

請填入正確的所有形容詞或所有格代名詞。

1. Ben and _____ friends have gone fishing. They have taken _____ fishing rods with them.

2. I told some of _____ friends the story but they said that no person in _____ right senses would believe me.

3. The woman groped _____ way toward the door. Suddenly a dog yelped in pain because she had stepped on _____ tail.

4. The cat has just had _____ meal but it seems to be hungry again.

5. The boy and _____ sister were catching butterflies in the garden when they saw a python. They ran to tell _____ father about it.

6. An uncle of _____ is coming to stay with us for a few days. We are all very excited about it.

7. The teacher told the students to write _____ names in _____ notebooks.

8. You must have left _____ pen at home. She certainly hasn't taken _____.

9. Lily borrowed _____ brother's badminton rackets because _____ was broken.

10. Have you seen _____ cat? I've been looking for it the whole day. It hasn't touched _____ food at all.

11. The boys offered me some of _____ candy and I gave them some of _____.

12. He applied for a job, but _____ application was turned down because _____ qualifications were not good enough.

13. The woman screamed when _____ gold chain was snatched from _____ neck. _____ cries alerted a policeman nearby.

14. We gave _____ books to them and they gave us _____ in exchange.

15. We have already had _____ baths but he hasn't had _____ yet. _____ friends will be coming over in a short while and he isn't even ready yet.

PART 12

請填入正確的所有形容詞或所有格代名詞。

1. He has sent _____ car to the garage for repairs. This car isn't _____; it's _____ cousin's.

2. I have lost _____ wallet. I don't think that I'll be able to find it, not even with _____ help. Moreover, you are in a hurry to go and I don't want to take up any more of _____ time.

3. If you have finished _____ painting, you can pack up _____ things now. Those who haven't finished _____ will have to stay behind.

4. May I borrow _____ razor? _____ is too blunt to be used.

5. Each of you should do _____ own work. Only when you have finished _____ can you help the others with _____.

6. A cousin of _____ came to visit us yesterday. He took us for a ride in _____ new

sports car.

7. It was raining heavily. As I hadn't brought _____ umbrella, I asked her to share _____ with me.

8. I met _____ friend by chance in a shop yesterday and we talked about _____ past schooldays. After that, she went _____ way and I went _____ .

9. Tony and _____ brother were on _____ way to the field to help _____ parents.

10. The tiger stalked _____ prey and pounced on it at the first opportunity.

11. All the dancers were ready and they took up _____ positions on the stage.

12. Mary and I tidied _____ room quickly and went downstairs to help _____ mother prepare breakfast.

13. _____ bicycle is of better quality than _____ . Where did you buy _____ ?

14. We were doing _____ homework in _____ room when Martin, a friend of _____ , rushed in.

15. The two boys have made up _____ minds to climb up to the top of the hill.

16. My sister refused to tell me _____ problem although I tried to offer her _____ help in solving it.

17. Barry has a very unusual stamp in _____ collection. He says that a businessman has offered him fifty thousand dollars for _____ stamp but he has refused to sell it.

18. "Is that _____ bicycle, Lawrence ?" "No, it isn't _____ . It's Rick's."

PART 13

請在空格中填入合適的不定形容詞（或不定代名詞）some 或 any。

1. _____ boys wanted to pick the pears on the tree but there weren't _____ ripe ones.

2. She wanted to eat _____ grapes but there weren't _____ left.

3. _____ plants can survive in places where there is hardly _____ water at all.

4. Did _____ of you let the cat into the bedroom?

5. She has bought _____ cloth. She is going to make shirts for everyone in the family.

6. She wants to boil _____ eggs, but there aren't _____ in the refrigerator.

7. I ate _____ sandwiches about ten minutes ago, and I don't feel like having _____ dinner now.

8. _____ of the neighbors helped him to carry the furniture into the house.

9. Pack _____ clothes into your suitcase.

10. She wanted to buy _____ pears, but there weren't _____ at the market.

11. She put _____ milk in her coffee but didn't want _____ sugar.

12. The shop doesn't sell _____ paint of this kind. You'll have to buy paint of _____ other kind.

13. May I have _____ coffee, please? I don't want _____ cakes.

14. They wanted _____ more food, but she refused to give them _____.

15. "Please do have _____ cookies if you don't want _____ more sandwiches," Mrs. Lee said.

16. The boys collected _____ dry sticks and made a fire to boil _____ water for tea.

17. My father has invited _____ friends to dinner. They may arrive at _____ moment now.

18. I don't have _____ stamps with me. But I can get you _____ on the way to school.

19. We had been hoping to see at least _____ of our friends at the party. But till the end, we did not meet _____ of them.

20. During the game _____ of the spectators became excited and noisy. They smashed bottles and tried to beat up _____ person who tried to stop them.

21. Did you meet anyone you know at the party? I'm sure _____ friends of yours were there.

PART 14

請在空格中填入合適的不定形容詞（或不定代名詞）some 或 any。

1. There were _____ CDs on the shelf, but he couldn't find _____ of those that he wanted to play.

2. I can't carry _____ more since both my hands are full.

3. We certainly don't need _____ more bread, but we do need _____ more butter.

4. Here are _____ jam tarts which I know you would like.

5. Please boil _____ more water. There isn't _____ left in the kettle.

6. Have you got _____ cakes left?

7. "Do have _____ soup," she urged me. "Put _____ pepper in it; it will add to the taste."

8. If you're going anywhere near the market, do get me _____ onions. There aren't

_____ left in the house.

9. It's a valuable stamp that he found on _____ old envelope. He hopes to get _____ money out of it.

10. Let's see if we can be of _____ help.

11. Last year, Mr. Fraser spent _____ time on a remote island in the Pacific. He did not meet anyone except for _____ fishermen.

12. "I'll be at home then," he said. "You can drop in at _____ time you like. I'll be glad to answer _____ queries that you may have."

13. A criminal broke out of prison _____ time last night. The police will welcome _____ information of his whereabouts.

14. We don't have _____ time to do anything further now. We'll continue at _____ other time.

15. I'm sure that I've seen that man before, but I don't have _____ clear recollection as to the exact place. Do you have _____ idea who he is?

16. There isn't _____ food left in the house. Could you go to the shop to buy _____?

17. _____ of the mangoes were sweet, _____ of them were sour, but there weren't _____ bad ones.

18. There are _____ lovely roses in your garden. But you don't have _____ carnations at all. I could give you _____ of mine.

19. We haven't had _____ news from him for _____ time. Maybe he is in _____ kind of trouble.

20. Terry did tell me something about the incident, but I didn't pay _____ attention to him.

21. We don't have _____ rice, but we do have _____ cakes and iced tea.

22. Someone broke into the house and made off with _____ money and _____ jewelry.

23. There may be _____ good cooks here, but there isn't anyone who can beat my mother in cookery. She makes _____ of the most delicious cakes I have ever tasted.

24. Hoping for a big trout, he pulled in the line only to find that he had caught _____ weeds. Sadly, he went home without _____ fish.

PART 15

請依題意在空格中填入 a few、a little、much 或 many 來完成句子。

1. I will not spend _____ money on the trip. _____ members of the society are going, and each will contribute _____ toward the cost of it.

2. She could not buy _____ apples from the lady because there were only _____ left.

3. We haven't got _____ bread left, but there is still _____ cheese in the refrigerator.

4. He can't find _____ time to do his homework these days. He has to attend sports practice _____ times a week.

5. The post office is just _____ kilometers away. It won't take you _____ time to walk there.

6. How _____ kilograms are there in a ton? Repeat the answer _____ times, and you'll remember it.

7. There aren't _____ old people in the audience tonight. Not _____ of them like to watch or listen to young people singing.

8. Please wait _____ while. He will be back from his office in just _____ minutes.

9. The food is tasteless. Can you please put _____ salt into it? Put in _____ pepper and _____ drops of tomato sauce, too.

10. Put _____ corn flour in the gravy to thicken it. Simmer the gravy for _____ minutes before taking it off the stove.

11. There are quite _____ old coins in my collection. I wonder how _____ they are worth now.

12. She has _____ more dresses to sew, but there is only _____ thread left on the reel.

13. Not _____ people attended the church wedding, but _____ turned up at the luncheon. We couldn't help feeling _____ disappointed at this attitude of the guests.

14. Use _____ ink-remover to get the stains off your shirt.

15. I will not take _____ of your time. I've got only _____ matters to clear up with you.

16. We couldn't buy _____ meat from the butcher as he had only _____ left.

PART 16

請依題意在空格中填入 a few、a little、much 或 many 來完成句子。

1. Dab _____ perfume behind your ears, but don't use too _____ as the scent can be overpowering.

2. _____ money is being spent to construct the road, which will be ready in _____

months' time.

3. How _____ days are there before the National Day celebrations? My brother can't help feeling _____ excited about taking part in the celebrations.

4. How _____ rice is there in the pot? We need only _____ to feed the cat.

5. There were not _____ oranges to choose from. We bought _____ which we thought were not sour.

6. There was only _____ space in the hole, but she managed to squeeze into it.

7. _____ of the rainwater has been drained away by the ditch.

8. She added _____ vanilla essence to the mixture.

9. There isn't _____ gasoline in the tank, so we'll have to stop at a gas station on the way.

10. How _____ work did he do and how _____ days did he take to do it?

11. There were _____ students loitering around the campus, so he called _____ of them to help him.

12. Not _____ traffic passes this way during the day, but at night _____ cars go to and fro.

13. There were _____ people living in those flats and _____ harm was done when the building collapsed.

Chapter 8 副　詞

8-1 副詞的構成

副詞可以由形容詞或其他詞類構成。

(a) 形容詞的字尾加上 ly，形成副詞。

USAGE PRACTICE

safe 安全的 → safe**ly** 安全地

bad 壞的 → bad**ly** 壞地

clear 清楚的 → clear**ly** 清楚地

careful 小心的 → careful**ly** 小心地

soft 柔軟的 → soft**ly** 柔軟地

deft 靈巧的 → deft**ly** 靈巧地

sole 單獨的 → sole**ly** 單獨地

youthful 年輕的 → youthful**ly** 年輕地

tired 疲倦的 → tired**ly** 疲倦地

rude 粗魯的 → rude**ly** 粗魯地

dear 親愛的 → dear**ly** 深情地

sudden 突然的 → sudden**ly** 突然地

worried 擔心的 → worried**ly** 擔心地

anxious 憂慮的 → anxious**ly** 憂慮地

laughing 可笑的 → laughing**ly** 可笑地

smiling 微笑的 → smiling**ly** 微笑地

real 真的 → real**ly** 真地

lawful 合法的 → lawful**ly** 合法地

skillful 熟練的 → skillful**ly** 熟練地

(b) 形容詞字尾是 y 者，去掉 y，再加上 ily，形成副詞。

USAGE PRACTICE

easy 容易的 → eas**ily** 容易地

angry 生氣的 → angr**ily** 生氣地

happy 快樂的 → happ**ily** 快樂地

merry 歡樂的 → merr**ily** 歡樂地

voluntary 自願的 → voluntar**ily** 自願地

weary 疲倦的 → wear**ily** 疲倦地

clumsy 笨拙的 → clums**ily** 笨拙地

lucky 幸運的 → luck**ily** 幸運地

steady 穩定的 → stead**ily** 穩定地

hearty 衷心的 → heart**ily** 衷心地

hungry 飢餓的 → hungr**ily** 飢餓地

(c) 形容詞字尾是 le 者，改為 ly，形成副詞。

USAGE PRACTICE

possible 可能的 → possib**ly** 可能地	simple 簡單的 → simp**ly** 簡單地
noble 高尚的 → nob**ly** 高尚地	idle 懶惰的 → id**ly** 懶惰地
probable 可能的 → probab**ly** 大概	feeble 虛弱的 → feeb**ly** 虛弱地
subtle 微妙的 → subt**ly** 微妙地	

 但是，也有例外的情況。

whole 全部的 → who**lly** 全部地

(d) 形容詞字尾是 ll 者，則加上 y，形成副詞。

USAGE PRACTICE

full 完全的 → full**y** 完全地	dull 乏味的 → dull**y** 遲鈍地

(e) 形容詞字尾是 ue 者，去掉 e，再加上 ly，形成副詞。

USAGE PRACTICE

true 真實的 → tru**ly** 真實地

(f) 形容詞字尾是 ic 者，則加上 ally，形成副詞。

USAGE PRACTICE

heroic 英雄的 → heroic**ally** 英雄地	tragic 悲劇的 → tragic**ally** 悲劇地
scientific 科學的 → scientific**ally** 科學地	comic 喜劇的 → comic**ally** 喜劇地
automatic 自動的 → automatic**ally** 自動地	
systematic 有系統的 → systematic**ally** 有系統地	
energetic 精力旺盛的 → energetic**ally** 精力旺盛地	

 但是，也有例外的情況。

public 公然的 → public**ly** 公然地

(g) 某些表示「方向」的副詞是以 way(s)、ward(s) 或 wise 結尾。

USAGE PRACTICE

side**ways** 向旁邊	up**ward(s)** 向上
back**ward(s)** 向後	sky**ward(s)** 朝天空
clock**wise** 順時針地	cross**wise** 交叉地

(h) 某些副詞是以 a 開頭。

USAGE PRACTICE

abroad 在國外	**a**loft 在高處	**a**shore 向岸上

(i) 許多副詞加上某些字首即可形成相反詞。

USAGE PRACTICE

uncertainly 猶豫不決地	**un**ceasingly 繼續地
unjustly 不公平地	**in**sanely 瘋狂地
insincerely 不誠摯地	**in**securely 不安全地
illegally 違法地	**ill**icitly 不正當地
illegibly 難讀地	**dis**pleasingly 令人不愉快地
disobediently 不服從地	**dis**reputably 名譽不好地

(j) 有些字本身可當形容詞，也可以當副詞，不需加字尾或字首來構成副詞。

USAGE PRACTICE

fast 迅速的／地	late 晚的／地	loud 大聲的／地
low 低的／地	hard 努力的／地	deep 深的／地
early 早的／地	high 高的／地	

形　容　詞	副　詞
a **fast** trip 很快完成的旅程	run **fast** 跑得快
a **hard** worker 努力的工人	work **hard** 努力工作
an **early** riser 早起的人	rise **early** 早起
a **daily** happening 每天發生的事	happen **daily** 每天發生

請寫出下列形容詞的副詞。

1. gradual _____
2. cheap _____
3. extreme _____
4. generous _____
5. probable _____
6. deliberate _____
7. regular _____
8. bold _____
9. terrible _____
10. lazy _____
11. rapid _____
12. punctual _____
13. happy _____
14. thoughtful _____
15. dramatic _____
16. slight _____
17. cruel _____
18. shameful _____
19. heavy _____
20. special _____
21. noble _____
22. sleepy _____
23. noisy _____
24. beautiful _____
25. sudden _____
26. brave _____
27. practical _____
28. pretty _____
29. hungry _____
30. miserable _____

☞ 更多相關習題請見本章應用練習 Part 1～Part 3。

8-2 副詞的種類

(a) 副詞有助於更生動地描述某動作或狀態，表達發生的方式、時間、地點等。副詞可分為五大類。

情狀副詞	politely 有禮貌地 softly 柔和地	loudly 大聲地	boldly 大膽地	bravely 勇敢地
地方副詞	here 這裡 everywhere 到處	inside 裡面 wherever 無論在哪裡	there 那裡	out 外面
時間副詞	now 現在 soon 不久	before 以前 ago 以前	then 那時 already 已經	today 今天 after 之後
程度副詞	very 非常 quite 相當 almost 幾乎 rather 頗	so 如此 even 甚至 simply 僅僅 just 只	merely 僅僅 fairly 非常 hardly 幾乎不	scarcely 幾乎不 nearly 幾乎 too 太
頻率副詞	always 總是 often 經常 twice 兩次	generally 通常 once 一次 occasionally 偶爾	regularly 規律地 seldom 很少 continually 持續不斷地	never 從不 sometimes 有時

(b) 有些副詞被用來加強語氣，這類副詞又稱為「語氣副詞」；其用法同於頻率副詞與程度副詞。

USAGE PRACTICE

surely 確實地	actually 事實上	truly 真正地
definitely 明確地	certainly 確實地	evidently 明顯地
utterly 完全地	distinctly 清楚地	positively 明確地
absolutely 絕對地	obviously 明顯地	

8-3 副詞的用法

(a) 副詞用來修飾動詞。

USAGE PRACTICE

▶ He spoke **rudely** to the old man. 他對老先生講話很無禮。

▶ The waitress smiled **pleasantly** at the customer. 女服務生愉快地對顧客微笑。

▶ She listened **carefully**. 她仔細地聆聽。

▶ She spoke **softly**. 她講話很輕柔。

▶ He ran **quickly** to the window. 他很快地跑到窗邊。

▶ They laughed **heartily** at the joke. 這個笑話讓他們盡情大笑。

▶ You must listen **attentively** to the teacher. 你必須注意地聽老師的話。

▶ She cried **bitterly** when she heard the news. 她聽到這個消息便痛哭失聲。

(b) 副詞用來修飾形容詞。

USAGE PRACTICE

▶ The old house was **clearly** visible from the road. 從馬路上就可以清楚看見那間舊房子。

▶ It was **extremely** cold last night. 昨晚天氣極冷。

▶ It is **highly** unlikely that anyone will believe his story. 不太可能有任何人會相信他的故事。

▶ He was **very** angry when I told him the news. 當我告訴他這個消息時，他非常生氣。

▶ Your dress is **too** short. 你的套裝太短了。

▶ It was **obviously** wrong, as we learned later. 後來我們得知那顯然是不對的。

▶ It is **really** remarkable the way they have organized everything.

他們把一切都組織起來的方法實在很了不起。

▶ The book was **too** thick. 這本書太厚了。

▶ We were **hardly** aware of the change in his behavior.

我們幾乎沒注意到他在行為方面的變化。

▶ This painting is **much** better than that one. 這幅畫比那幅畫好多了。

(c) 副詞用來修飾副詞。

USAGE PRACTICE

▶ He walked **very** slowly out of the room. 他非常慢地走出房間。

▶ He fell **quite** heavily from the tree and broke his leg. 他從樹上重重摔下，摔斷了腿。

▶ They have thought **very** deeply about this matter. 他們已經非常深入地想過這件事。

▶ He behaved **extremely** well yesterday. 他昨天表現得極好。

(d) 副詞用來修飾句子。

USAGE PRACTICE

Fortunately, he was there to help us. 幸好他在那裡幫助我們。

請選擇適當的副詞填入空格中。

patiently	loudly	badly	accidentally
generously	fluently	skillfully	heavily
nervously	fiercely	gently	early
dearly	punctually	safely	now
well	politely	regularly	

1. We waited _____ for them.

2. She spilled the milk _____ .

3. If you ring the door bell _____ , they will wake up.

4. They arrived at the school _____ today. It was only seven o'clock then.

5. He was _____ injured in the accident.

6. The millionaire _____ gave the money to the charity.

7. The train reached its destination _____ .

8. He fell so _____ from the tree that he broke his leg.

9. _____ the nurse washed the wound and _____ bandaged it up after she had applied ointment to it.

10. She attended French classes _____, which is why she can speak _____ in that language now.

11. The policeman inquired _____ whether he had come to the right house.

12. The dog barked _____ at the visitor who stood _____ at the entrance of the house.

13. They should be _____ home by now!

14. She is in the hall _____ . She is _____ dressed.

15. His parents love him _____ as he is their only child.

☞ 更多相關習題請見本章應用練習 Part 4。

8-4 副詞的位置

(a) 情狀副詞用來描述某一動作如何進行，通常放在動詞的後面。

USAGE PRACTICE

▶ He chuckled **merrily** at the joke. 這個笑話使他開心地咯咯笑。

▶ They slept **soundly** last night. 他們昨晚睡得很熟。

▶ She sang **sweetly**. 她甜美地唱歌。

▶ He whistled **cheerfully** as he walked along the road.

　他一邊開心地吹著口哨，一邊沿著馬路走。

▶ They laughed **heartily** at the boy's mistake. 他們恣意地嘲笑男孩所犯的錯誤。

▶ He ran **swiftly** to the hospital. 他很快地跑到醫院。

 情狀副詞也可以放在直接受詞的後面。換言之，當受詞緊接在動詞後時，副詞絕對不可置於動詞與受詞之間。

▶ He sent an email **immediately** to his nephew. 他立刻寄電子郵件給他的侄子。

▶ He passed the ball **quickly** to the captain. 他很快地把球傳給隊長。

▶ The men finished their meal **quickly**. 男士們很快地把他們的餐點吃完。

▶ He treated the boy **well**. 他對這男孩很好。

▶ He greeted his guests **politely**. 他有禮地問候他的客人。

▶ She read the letter **loudly**. 她很大聲地讀這封信。

▶ He beat the boy **brutally**. 他很粗暴地打這男孩。

▶ He shut the door **angrily**. 他很生氣地關上門。

> **但是我們會用**
>
> ▶ He fought **bravely** against the current. 他勇敢地對抗潮流。
> ▶ She spoke **softly** to the weeping child. 她輕柔地對哭泣的孩子說話。
> ▶ The cat cried **pitifully** for milk. 小貓很可憐地叫著要奶喝。

★情狀副詞可以置於動詞與介系詞之間。

(b) 程度副詞通常放在動詞之前，或者放在助動詞和一般動詞之間。

USAGE PRACTICE

▶ I **scarcely** paid attention to what they were saying. 我幾乎沒注意到他們在說什麼。

▶ We **quite** understand the situation. 我們相當了解這狀況。

▶ She **almost** missed the train. 她差點趕不上火車。

▶ She had **almost** finished when I entered. 當我進去時，她幾乎已經完成了。

(c) 地方副詞用來表達某一動作發生的地方，通常放在動詞的後面；若有直接受詞時，則放在直接受詞的後面。

USAGE PRACTICE

▶ He went **inside**. 他進去裡面了。

▶ Did they go **there**? 他們去了那裡嗎？

▶ We went **everywhere** by bus. 我們到哪都搭公車。

▶ He came **here** at nine o'clock. 他九點來到這裡。

▶ She has put the chair **here** for you. 她已經為你把椅子擺在這裡。

▶ She drove the car **here**. 她開車來這裡。

▶ The parents sent all their children **home**. 家長把他們所有的小孩都送回家。

▶ My brother drove him **here**. 我哥哥開車載他來這裡。

(d) 時間副詞用來表達某一動作在何時發生，通常放在句首或句尾。

▶ A thief broke into the house **last night**. 昨晚有小偷闖入屋內。

▶ **Yesterday**, the Smiths came here for a visit. 昨天，史密斯一家人來這裡拜訪。

▶ He was here **a moment ago**. 他片刻之前還在這裡。

▶ **Soon afterward**, they set off for the soccer game. 不久之後，他們出發去看足球賽。

▶ Do you want to go **now**? 你現在想離開嗎？

▶ **Soon** we will have to go. 不久我們就得離開了。

▶ **Every morning** we get up as early as we can. 每天早上我們都儘可能地早起。

▶ I'll visit you again **next Monday**. 我下星期一將再次拜訪你。

(e) 當兩個以上的副詞或副詞片語一起使用時，通常依下列順序排列：狀態→地點→時間。但是，這順序並非一成不變，可以視需要而調整。

S + V (+ O)	狀　態	地　點	時　間
She signed her name （她簽名）	neatly （整齊地）	in the book （在書裡）	just now. （剛才）
He had been sleeping （他已經睡了）	soundly （很熟地）	in the room （在房裡）	for two hours. （兩小時）
The kitten was playing （小貓在玩耍）	happily （快樂地）	under the bed （在床下）	all afternoon. （整個下午）
He fell （他摔下來）	heavily （重重地）	from the tree （從樹上）	yesterday. （昨天）
I saw a film （我看電影）		at the Odeon Cinema （在奧地昂電影院）	last night. （昨晚）
She sang （她唱歌）	sweetly （甜美地）	at the concert （在演唱會中）	last night. （昨晚）
The man walked （這男人走路）	like a drunk （像醉漢似地）	along the road （沿著馬路）	yesterday. （昨天）

 有許多表示「地點」和「時間」的副詞片語是由介系詞與名詞構成。

| on the desk 在書桌上 | to the end of the road 到馬路的盡頭 | |
| in the morning 在早上 | at that day 在那一天 | since 1972 從1972年以來 |

(f) 副詞 enough 總是放在被它修飾的形容詞或副詞之後。

USAGE PRACTICE

▶ He wasn't <u>lucky</u> **enough** to win a prize. 他運氣不夠好，無法得獎。

▶ The bullfighter didn't move <u>swiftly</u> **enough**. 鬥牛士移動得不夠迅速。

(g) 副詞 only 置於它所修飾的字旁邊。在以下這些句子裡，請注意 only 的位置不同，意義也有差異。

USAGE PRACTICE

▶ He **only** <u>lent</u> the book to me. 他只是把這本書借給我。

▶ He lent **only** <u>the book</u> to me. 他只借這本書給我。(他沒借我其它東西)

▶ He lent the book to <u>me</u> **only**. 他這本書只借給我。(沒借給其他人)

小練習

請依正確的順序加上副詞或副詞片語以完成句子。

1. The team practiced (*on the school field; hard; all day*).

   → _____

2. I have been (*several times; to Skyline Beach; this month*).

   → _____

3. This area is (*for eight hours; daily; under curfew*).

   → _____

4. She missed her parents (*while they were abroad; badly; last month*).

   → _____

5. She sang (*last evening; beautifully; in the contest*).

   → _____

6. The baby was crying (*in the next room; the whole of last night; loudly*).

   → _____

7. They broke the news to her (*when she came back; gently; yesterday*).

$\rightarrow$ _____

8. He shouted (*over the telephone; loudly*).

$\rightarrow$ _____

9. They were talking (*by the door; when I came upon them; in low tones*).

$\rightarrow$ _____

10. The taxi stopped (*just now; suddenly; at the curb*).

$\rightarrow$ _____

11. My uncle has been thinking it over (*in his office; carefully; for days*).

$\rightarrow$ _____

12. He tiptoed (*into the room; quietly; last night*) and went to bed.

$\rightarrow$ _____

13. Did you water the plants (*in my absence; regularly*)?

$\rightarrow$ _____

14. The train came (*at one o'clock; into the station*), and it left (*an hour ago; for Citiland*).

$\rightarrow$ _____

☞ 更多相關習題請見本章應用練習 Part 5～Part 9。

8-5 頻率副詞

(a) 頻率副詞用來表達「某一事情發生次數的多寡」。

USAGE PRACTICE			
always 總是	seldom 很少	often 常常	frequently 經常
continually 不時地	regularly 定期地	sometimes 有時	generally 通常地
never 從不	usually 經常	rarely 不常地	occasionally 偶爾地

(b) 頻率副詞必須置於 be 動詞的後面。

USAGE PRACTICE
▶ He was **usually** late for work. 他經常上班遲到。
▶ They are **usually** at Mary's house at this time of the day. 白天這個時候他們通常在瑪麗的家。

▶ He is **always** at the swimming pool on Saturdays.　星期六他總是在游泳池。

▶ She was **seldom** out of the house.　她很少出門。

▶ She is **seldom** at home.　她很少待在家。

▶ There was **seldom** any food in the house.　房子裡很少有食物。

▶ He is **sometimes** wrong in his judgment.　他有時候判斷錯誤。

▶ She is **often** upset these days.　這幾天她經常感到心煩。

(c) 頻率副詞通常位於一般動詞的前面。

USAGE PRACTICE

▶ It **sometimes** rains in the evenings.　晚上有時候會下雨。

▶ He **rarely** wears a tie now.　他現在很少打領帶。

▶ He **rarely** plays with his younger brothers.　他很少跟弟弟們玩。

▶ I **often** go to bed at ten o'clock.　我常常十點就寢。

▶ They **seldom** do their homework.　他們很少做他們的家庭作業。

▶ I **seldom** hear her apologize for anything.　我很少聽到她為任何事情道歉。

▶ The children **usually** come here in the evenings.　孩子們經常在晚上來這裡。

▶ I **usually** visit my uncle during the holidays.　我常在假日時拜訪我叔叔。

▶ He **never** goes to the clinic by himself.　他從來沒有單獨一個人去過診所。

▶ She **always** does her work neatly.　她總是把她的工作做得很好。

但是我們會用
▶ He smokes **occasionally** at the office.　他在辦公室偶爾會抽煙。

★少數頻率副詞會置於一般動詞之後。

(d) 頻率副詞通常置於助動詞與一般動詞之間。

USAGE PRACTICE

▶ They will **never** find the treasure.　他們將永遠找不到寶藏。

▶ You must **never** cheat anyone.　你絕對不可欺騙任何人。

▶ My stepmother has **never** understood me.　我的繼母從來沒有了解過我。

▶ She has **always** been successful in the examinations.　她的考試成績通常很好。

▶ I might **sometimes** go to the movies.　我可能偶爾會去看電影。

▶ Michael and Frank are **rarely** seen in town nowadays.

現在很少在鎮上看見邁可和法蘭克。

▶ He should **regularly** do some exercise. 他應該規律性地做些運動。

 但是，若想要強調副詞時，可以置於助動詞之前。

▶ She **never** can understand what I say. 她從來不能理解我説的話。

▶ I **always** have come here and I will continue to do so. 我總是來這裡，而且將會繼續下去。

請在正確的位置加上頻率副詞以完成句子。

1. He will realize his mistake. (*never*)

   → _____

2. She has been kind to us. (*always*)

   → _____

3. Customers are hard to please. (*generally*)

   → _____

4. That country has been under foreign rule. (*never*)

   → _____

5. The turtles come to lay their eggs on the beach. (*sometimes*)

   → _____

6. A tiger kills a human being. (*seldom*)

   → _____

7. He is absent from school. (*frequently*)

   → _____

8. Have you been to Italy? (*ever*)

   → _____

9. You must wash your hands before you eat. (*always*)

   → _____

10. Mosquitoes are found in swampy areas. (*usually*)

   → _____

11. We write letters these days. (*seldom*)

→ _____

12. They have been to the zoo before. (*never*)

→ _____

13. The farmers harvest their crops in August. (*usually*)

→ _____

14. Will she learn how to tie her shoelaces? (*ever*)

→ _____

15. Do you plan your composition before you write it? (*generally*)

→ _____

16. These birds are seen outside the jungle. (*rarely*)

→ _____

17. We eat out in the evenings. (*sometimes*)

→ _____

18. Why does Sally come to school late? (*always*)

→ _____

19. Have you thought about going on a round-the-world trip? (*ever*)

→ _____

20. I will remember what happened at the seaside that day. (*always*)

→ _____

☞ 更多相關習題請見本章應用練習 Part 10～Part 12。

8-6 副詞的倒裝

(a) 倒裝用法是指將動詞或助動詞置於主詞之前。使用於倒裝句的副詞常常被置於句首，用來加強語氣，且常帶有否定或其他意思。

USAGE PRACTICE

▶ **Never** have I done such a thing before. 我以前從未做過這樣的事情。

▶ **Seldom** does he show much improvement. 他很少表現出很大的進步。

▶ **Nowhere** else in the world can you find such a multiracial society.
你在世上任何地方都無法找到這樣多民族融合的社會。

基礎文法寶典 ❷
Essential English Usage & Grammar

▶ **No longer** will I trust you. 我再也不會信任你了。

▶ **So** diligently did the boys work that they finished before the date due.

這些男孩們工作地如此勤奮以至於他們在到期之前就完成了。

▶ **So** clearly did he explain the lesson that everyone understood it.

他將這一課解釋得如此清楚以至於大家都懂了。

▶ Just as you have done yours, **so** will I do mine. 就像你已經做了你的工作，我也會做我的。

▶ **Helplessly** did the new teacher stare at the noisy students.

這新老師無助地盯著這群吵鬧的學生。

▶ **Deep** in her mind is her fear of the dark. 在內心深處她是怕黑的。

▶ **Only** with supervision would he do his work neatly.

只有在監督下，他才會好好地做他的工作。

 小練習

請將下列句子的副詞移到句首，形成倒裝句。

1. He will understand the hardships of working for a living only when he grows up.

   → _____

2. She has rarely failed in her examinations.

   → _____

3. I have never in my life heard of such injustice.

   → _____

4. They have seldom been so late for the meeting.

   → _____

5. The girls begged so earnestly that their mother gave them what they wanted.

   → _____

6. I will never again do that without asking your advice first.

   → _____

7. You will hardly ever see old Mr. Jolly without a smile on his face.

   → _____

8. They did their work so quietly that the teacher suspected some mischief.

   → _____

9. The father spanked his son soundly.

→ _____

10. He realized that the child would perform his task only with supervision.

→ _____

Chapter 8　應用練習

PART 1

請寫出下列形容詞的副詞。

1. glad _____
2. skilful _____
3. wise _____
4. safe _____
5. polite _____
6. fierce _____
7. free _____
8. swift _____
9. serious _____
10. untidy _____
11. dear _____
12. painful _____
13. joyful _____
14. clumsy _____
15. actual _____
16. bad _____
17. nice _____
18. loud _____
19. forceful _____
20. busy _____

PART 2

請寫出下列形容詞的副詞。

1. continual _____
2. efficient _____
3. essential _____
4. annoying _____
5. fixed _____
6. real _____
7. possible _____
8. whole _____
9. due _____
10. deep _____
11. quarter _____
12. frantic _____
13. personal _____
14. surprising _____
15. useless _____
16. usual _____
17. minute _____
18. relative _____
19. humble _____
20. right _____
21. high _____
22. annual _____
23. mechanic _____
24. sheepish _____
25. joking _____
26. weary _____
27. healthy _____
28. suspicious _____
29. hasty _____
30. energetic _____
31. boyish _____
32. wooden _____
33. satisfactory _____
34. quick _____
35. testy _____
36. voluble _____

37. loyal _____

PART 3

請寫出下列形容詞的副詞。

1. industrious _____   2. foggy _____   3. girlish _____

4. gigantic _____   5. sunny _____   6. systematic _____

7. attentive _____   8. graceful _____   9. analytical _____

10. useful _____   11. studious _____   12. memorable _____

13. periodic _____   14. perfect _____   15. perceptible _____

16. kind _____   17. lucky _____   18. favorable _____

19. peremptory _____   20. noticeable _____   21. horrible _____

22. simple _____   23. inane _____   24. excited _____

25. inaudible _____   26. monstrous _____   27. noble _____

28. legible _____   29. daily _____   30. objective _____

PART 4

請依提示在適當的位置加入副詞以完成句子。

1. We can harvest the crop faster if we use that kind of machine. (*even*)

    → _____

2. This is the most impressive sculpture in the exhibition. (*quite*)

    → _____

3. I was sorry to hear of the tragic accident. (*extremely*)

    → _____

4. He has taken a few swimming lessons and he can swim well now. (*fairly*)

    → _____

5. This is the best film that I have ever seen. (*definitely*)

    → _____

6. The quality of this material is superior to that. (*distinctly*)

    → _____

7. You are correct in your diagnosis. (*perfectly*)

    → _____

8. It is right that he should apologize to his cousin. (*only*)

→ _____

9. The crates of smuggled wine were concealed among the bushes. (*partly*)

→ _____

10. This box is not big for us to put all these things in. (*enough*)

→ _____

11. The picture that he recently drew is the best in the collection. (*quite*)

→ _____

12. We were sorry when we found out that we had accused him wrongly. (*deeply*)

→ _____

13. He didn't work quickly; that's why he was late. (*enough*)

→ _____

14. They believed half of what I said. (*only*)

→ _____

15. We were dumbfounded when we saw him again. (*utterly*)

→ _____

16. The jug was empty when I first looked in it. Now it is full. (*practically; almost*)

→ _____

17. The village has changed during the past few years. I can believe that it could change so fast. (*enormously; scarcely*)

→ _____

18. "The fault is yours." "No, it isn't. You are at fault." (*entirely; equally*)

→ _____

19. This house isn't big to accommodate fifteen people. We need a bigger house. (*enough; much*)

→ _____

PART 5

請依正確的順序加上副詞或副詞片語以完成句子。

1. It had been raining. (*here; continuously; for the past week*)

→ _____

2. He lighted the firecracker. (*just now; carefully*)

→ _____

3. They shouted when they heard his call. (*last night; from the window; noisily*)

   → _____

4. The wind was blowing. (*from the north; strongly*)

   → _____

5. She is seated. (*beside the man; in front*)

   → _____

6. The workmen were chatting with each other. (*all yesterday afternoon; happily*)

   → _____

7. The children are hanging up their stockings. (*tonight; in their rooms*)

   → _____

8. The train came. (*punctually; at nine o'clock; into the station*)

   → _____

9. The taxi driver braked. (*in front of the church; noisily*)

   → _____

10. They have been up. (*twice; since last January; Mount Fuji*)

    → _____

11. The baby had been sleeping. (*in the next room; soundly; for a few hours*)

    → _____

12. He had been ringing the doorbell. (*insistently; for about ten minutes*)

    → _____

13. The woman scolded the boy. (*in the garden; angrily; last night*)

    → _____

14. The ship sailed. (*yesterday morning; at six o'clock; for Sri Lanka*)

    → _____

15. The typhoon destroyed many houses. (*last month; on the island*)

    → _____

PART 6

請依正確的順序加上副詞或副詞片語以完成句子。

1. I watered the plants (*on the front porch; before having my dinner*).

→ _____

2. The boy laughed (*when he heard that; last night; heartily*).

→ _____

3. They had been discussing the matter (*thoroughly; for half an hour; before casting the vote*).

→ _____

4. He got off the bus (*at the bus stop; rather clumsily*).

→ _____

5. Does she have to go (*to Sun Island; immediately; with all of us*)?

→ _____

6. Peter and Paul came here (*by bus; rather unexpectedly; yesterday evening*).

→ _____

7. The car was damaged (*yesterday; very badly; in the accident*).

→ _____

8. Aunt Polly put all the clothes (*neatly; after folding them; into the cupboard*).

→ _____

9. A man grabbed me (*roughly; as I was passing by; on the dark street*).

→ _____

10. The doorbell has been ringing (*the whole day; on and off*).

→ _____

11. The policeman was whistling (*as he cycled along the road; early in the morning; softly*).

→ _____

12. She gave me a gift (*during my birthday party; with a shy smile; at my home*).

→ _____

13. They offered to give me a lift (*willingly; in the mornings; to my office*).

→ _____

14. We witnessed a serious accident (*last week; at the intersection; near the market*).

→ _____

PART 7

請依正確的順序加上副詞或副詞片語以完成句子。

1. He pushed me (*out of the way; roughly*).

→ _____

2. John and Tom came home (*with some friends; unexpectedly; this morning*).

→ _____

3. She put on her make-up (*in front of the mirror; after breakfast; carefully*).

→ _____

4. They were watching television (*last night; when we came home; quietly*).

→ _____

5. I did not go (*yesterday morning; to the movies; with my friends*).

→ _____

6. The teacher scolded the naughty boy (*this morning; severely; in class*).

→ _____

7. They saw a frightening film (*terribly; last week; at the Odeon*).

→ _____

8. The students started giggling (*rather childishly; when they heard the story*).

→ _____

9. I packed all the clothes (*into the suitcases; neatly; after ironing them*).

→ _____

10. Do we have to tell them the news (*at Mary's house; when we meet them*)?

→ _____

11. The naughty boy fell (*while watching the parade; rather heavily; from the wall*).

→ _____

12. Helen and her sisters had intended to go shopping (*this morning; along Trenton Street*).

→ _____

13. It hasn't been raining (*in this region; at all; for the past two months*).

→ _____

14. Somebody has been trying to reach you (*the whole day; on the telephone; urgently*).

→ _____

15. The girl accepted their good wishes and congratulations (*at her birthday party; with a modest smile; last night*).

→ _____

PART 8

請依正確的順序加上副詞或副詞片語以完成句子。

1. He wanted to do that (*very much; all his life*).

   → _____

2. She is going (*on Monday; to Sydney; for two weeks*).

   → _____

3. The students stayed (*all morning; quietly; in class*).

   → _____

4. That old woman was born (*in the year 1890; at four o'clock; on Christmas morning*).

   → _____

5. He has worked (*throughout the week; very hard; in class*).

   → _____

6. She danced (*at the City Hall; last week; gracefully; in the concert*).

   → _____

7. Shall I meet you (*outside the movie theater; on Tuesday; at noon*)?

   → _____

8. He spoke to us (*on our way to school; rudely; this morning*).

   → _____

9. The boy grinned when he met us (*at the candy shop; sheepishly*).

   → _____

10. He swerved when he rounded the corner (*to the pavement; violently*).

    → _____

11. I bought a pair of shoes (*last Saturday; in that shop; at the annual sale*).

    → _____

12. He arrived (*at the office; late; this morning*).

    → _____

13. The beggar told his tale as he sat on the sidewalk (*pitifully; every day*).

    → _____

14. The boy chased the goats (*when he saw them eating the plants; angrily; out of the garden*).

    → _____

15. The runners ran (*around the field; during the race; as fast as they could*).

→ _____

16. He listens to the teacher (*in the class; attentively; every day*).

   → _____

17. The car ran over the dog while it was running across the road (*accidentally; a few minutes ago*).

   → _____

18. I do my homework (*always; in my room; in the afternoon*).

   → _____

19. He rebuked the boy (*yesterday; loudly; when he saw him bullying another boy*).

   → _____

20. The robbery took place (*in the afternoon; in the Galaxy Goldsmith shop; at two o'clock*).

   → _____

PART 9

請依正確的順序加上副詞或副詞片語以完成句子。

1. We went (*last night; to the movies*).

   → _____

2. The jockeys led their horses (*when the order was given; to the racetrack*).

   → _____

3. The Russian troupe performed (*at the Cultural Hall; excellently, last month*).

   → _____

4. The dog barked (*last night; loudly; when I opened the gate*).

   → _____

5. We have tea (*every day; under the tree; in the garden*).

   → _____

6. We went (*after work; home; immediately*).

   → _____

7. The sheep protested (*when the shearers started working on them; noisily*).

   → _____

8. Mike has acted (*since the day that he saw the accident; in a strange manner*).

   → _____

9. He scolded the boy (*when he caught him stealing the fruit; angrily; yesterday*).

→ _____

10. Peter shouted "Fire! Fire!" (*last night; when he saw smoke coming out of the house; loudly*).

→ _____

11. The accident occurred (*in the afternoon; outside the hospital*).

→ _____

12. The "lion dance" was performed (*outside the town hall; last Sunday*).

→ _____

13. The children were playing (*in the shallow river; joyfully; when it started to rain*).

→ _____

14. The man talked (*at the dinner; eloquently*).

→ _____

15. A stranger came up to us (*as we were walking home; suddenly; last night*).

→ _____

16. The acrobat jumped (*nimbly; over the wall; when he heard a cry for help*).

→ _____

17. The boy helped the blind man (*across the street; carefully; just now*).

→ _____

18. The twins were born (*in 1960; at four o'clock; on New Year's Day; at the District Hospital*).

→ _____

19. The guard crept (*around the office building; when he heard some sounds; cautiously*).

→ _____

20. The athlete threw the javelin (*last week; as far as he could; at the sports meet*).

→ _____

PART 10

請在正確的位置加上頻率副詞以完成句子。

1. He has met with an accident in his car before. (*never*)

→ _____

2. These boys are punished for their mistakes. (*always*)

→ _____

3. The train is delayed these days. (*often*)

→ _____

4. He sets mousetraps in his house. (*sometimes*)

→ _____

5. Her relatives stay until the visiting hours are over. (*usually*)

→ _____

6. Has he been to Windy Hill? (*ever*)

→ _____

7. Parents are invited to the prize-giving ceremony each year. (*always*)

→ _____

8. Frogs come out after it rains. (*usually*)

→ _____

9. The shops are full of customers on Saturdays. (*generally*)

→ _____

10. He loses his temper with his children. (*rarely*)

→ _____

11. She sleeps on the top bunk. (*sometimes*)

→ _____

12. "Have you seen a gold coin?" (*ever*) "No, I have seen one." (*never*)

→ _____

13. This kind of bird is seen near where people live. (*rarely*)

→ _____

14. Tourists stay in that hotel. (*usually*)

→ _____

15. He forgets to lock his room before he goes out. (*sometimes*)

→ _____

16. That boy forgets when the meetings are supposed to begin. (*always*)

→ _____

17. The boys have been punished for ill-treating the neighbors' cats. (*occasionally*)

→ _____

18. Do they swim in that stream near the edge of the jungle? (*frequently*)

→ _____

19. His mother has told him not to play in the street. (*often*)

→ _____

20. This is the first time anyone has treated me this way. (*ever*)

→ _____

PART 11

請在正確的位置加上頻率副詞以完成句子。

1. You see such good performances in circuses of this type. (*rarely*)

→ _____

2. I manage to reach home in time to watch my favorite television program. (*nearly always*)

→ _____

3. She does everything neatly; she is untidy, and she makes a place dirty. (*always; never; seldom*)

→ _____

4. They pass her house on their way to school. (*usually*)

→ _____

5. Do you know why Robert comes to school late? (*always*)

→ _____

6. They had been waiting for over an hour when we arrived. (*already*)

→ _____

7. I have enjoyed myself so much at a party as I've done at this one. (*seldom*)

→ _____

8. These girls are punctual when there is a meeting. (*never*)

→ _____

9. The absent-minded old man sends his letters to the wrong addresses. (*frequently*)

→ _____

10. Her mother has told her never to go home later than ten; but she obeys. (*repeatedly; seldom*)

→ _____

11. He visits his Aunt Sally, but he drops in at Aunt Mary's house. (*rarely; frequently*)

→ _____

12. "Has your pressure cooker given you any trouble?" "No, it hasn't. It runs smoothly." (*ever;

always)

→ _____

13. I do not remember having met him. (*ever*)

→ _____

14. He has been disobedient. (*occasionally*)

→ _____

15. We see him these days. (*seldom*)

→ _____

16. He has been here but he hardly remembers anything. (*twice*)

→ _____

17. None of us had been there before. (*ever*)

→ _____

18. You should do as your elders tell you. (*always*)

→ _____

19. You must get off a bus when it is moving. (*never*)

→ _____

20. I would have known what to do if you had not guided me. (*never; always*)

→ _____

PART 12

請在正確的位置加上頻率副詞以完成句子。

1. That scientist goes to bed at four in the morning. (*usually*)

→ _____

2. I have been told to report to him. (*often*)

→ _____

3. She has been there before. (*never*)

→ _____

4. He is at home. (*scarcely ever*)

→ _____

5. He has lunch in the office. (*occasionally*)

→ _____

6. Mr. Lewis smiles at us these days. (*rarely*)

→ _____

7. You will see such a sight again. (*never*)

→ _____

8. The old woman visits her doctor. (*regularly*)

→ _____

9. He has done such a thing before. (*never*)

→ _____

10. He was absent from work in the mine. (*seldom*)

→ _____

11. This is the most memorable day in my life; I will remember it. (*always*)

→ _____

12. The President is accompanied by his bodyguards. (*often*)

→ _____

13. "Do you read in bed?" (*always*) "Yes, I do." (*always*)

→ _____

14. I get up with the dawn. (*generally*)

→ _____

15. The doctor advised the old woman to take her medicine. (*always; regularly*)

→ _____

16. I have told him not to play in the rain but he does. (*repeatedly; nearly always*)

→ _____

17. Previously he had nightmares and now he has them. (*often; occasionally*)

→ _____

18. Don't do that again; you cannot get away with it. (*ever; always*)

→ _____

19. I walk in the woods by myself and after these walks I feel happier. (*sometimes; generally*)

→ _____

Chapter 9 形容詞與副詞的比較

9-1 形容詞的比較

形容詞的比較有三級：原級、比較級與最高級。比較級和最高級是由原級所構成。

(a) 大部分單音節或部分雙音節的形容詞在字尾加上 er（結尾字母為 e 時，則只加 r）構成比較級，加上 est（結尾字母為 e 時，則只加 st）構成最高級。

原　　級	比　較　級	最　高　級
small 小的	smaller 較小的	smallest 最小的
high 高的	higher 較高的	highest 最高的
gentle 溫和的	gentler 較溫和的	gentlest 最溫和的
loud 大聲的	louder 較大聲的	loudest 最大聲的
short 短的	shorter 較短的	shortest 最短的
clever 聰明的	cleverer 較聰明的	cleverest 最聰明的
hard 困難的	harder 較困難的	hardest 最困難的
long 長的	longer 較長的	longest 最長的
fast 快的	faster 較快的	fastest 最快的
wise 有智慧的	wiser 較有智慧的	wisest 最有智慧的

 注意　字尾是 y 時，要刪掉 y，再加上 ier 構成比較級，或加上 iest 構成最高級。

原級	比較級	最高級
lazy 懶惰的	lazier 較懶惰的	laziest 最懶惰的
merry 歡樂的	merrier 較歡樂的	merriest 最歡樂的
early 早的	earlier 較早的	earliest 最早的
easy 容易的	easier 較容易的	easiest 最容易的

(b) 大部分兩個以上音節的形容詞，加上 more 構成比較級，加上 most 構成最高級。

原　　級	比　較　級	最　高　級
reluctant 不情願的	**more** reluctant 較不情願的	**most** reluctant 最不情願的
risky 有風險的	**more** risky 較有風險的	**most** risky 最有風險的

comfortable 舒適的	**more** comfortable 較舒適的	**most** comfortable 最舒適的
famous 有名的	**more** famous 較有名的	**most** famous 最有名的
selfish 自私的	**more** selfish 較自私的	**most** selfish 最自私的
stupid 愚蠢的	**more** stupid 較愚蠢的	**most** stupid 最愚蠢的
beautiful 美麗的	**more** beautiful 較美麗的	**most** beautiful 最美麗的
interesting 有趣的	**more** interesting 較有趣的	**most** interesting 最有趣的
hopeful 有希望的	**more** hopeful 較有希望的	**most** hopeful 最有希望的
fertile 肥沃的	**more** fertile 較肥沃的	**most** fertile 最肥沃的

(c) 還有一些形容詞比較級和最高級的構成屬於不規則變化。

原　級	比　較　級	最　高　級
bad 壞的	worse 較壞的	worst 最壞的
good 好的	better 較好的	best 最好的
many/much 多的	more 較多的	most 最多的
little 少的	less 較少的	least 最少的
late 遲的	later/latter 較遲的／後者的	latest/last 最遲的／最後的
far 遠的	farther/further 更遠的／更進一步的	farthest/furthest 最遠的

(d) 某些形容詞沒有比較級或最高級。

USAGE PRACTICE			
perfect 完美的	empty 空的	unique 獨特的	round 圓的
square 方形的	universal 普遍的	circular 圓形的	daily 每天的

小練習

請依最合理的句子情境，寫出所提示形容詞的比較級或最高級。

1. She has just taken a sleeping tablet. She is feeling _____ (*drowsy*) every minute now.

2. Who is _____ (*young*), John or David?

3. He is one of the _____ (*wealthy*) men in the world.

4. Nora was _____ (*surprised*) at his appearance than you were.

5. He looked _____ (*pale*) and _____ (*thin*) after his illness. Before, he weighed the _____ (*heavy*) among the three of us, but now he is even _____ (*light*) than I am.

6. The soup is _____ (*tasty*) than the vegetables.

7. She is _____ (*successful*) than her brother.

8. The _____ (*little*) you can do is to help her find a room to stay in.

9. You have _____ (*much*) money than you need for the trip. The _____ (*much*) you need to spend is about three hundred dollars.

10. The crust is the _____ (*hard*) but the _____ (*delicious*) part of the bread.

11. This chair is _____ (*comfortable*) than that one, but it is _____ (*expensive*), too.

12. His condition today has become _____ (*bad*) than yesterday.

13. The _____ (*good*) part of the film is when the hero slays his _____ (*bitter*) enemy and wins back the heroine.

14. We have decided on the _____ (*easy*) way to deal with this problem. However, we will be _____ (*confident*) if you will give us your _____ (*full*) support.

9-2 副詞的比較

(a) 單音節和部分雙音節的副詞在字尾加 er 構成比較級，加 est 構成最高級。

原　級	比　較　級	最　高　級
soon 快地	soon**er** 較快地	soon**est** 最快地
fast 快地	fast**er** 較快地	fast**est** 最快地
hard 努力地	hard**er** 較努力地	hard**est** 最努力地

(b) 兩個或兩個以上音節的副詞，加上 more 構成比較級，加上 most 構成最高級。

原　級	比　較　級	最　高　級
selfishly 自私地	**more** selfishly 較自私地	**most** selfishly 最自私地
easily 容易地	**more** easily 較容易地	**most** easily 最容易地

bravely 英勇地	**more** bravely 較英勇地	**most** bravely 最英勇地
diligently 勤勉地	**more** diligently 較勤勉地	**most** diligently 最勤勉地
hopefully 有希望地	**more** hopefully 較有希望地	**most** hopefully 最有希望地
cowardly 膽小地	**more** cowardly 較膽小地	**most** cowardly 最膽小地
freely 自由地	**more** freely 較自由地	**most** freely 最自由地
angrily 生氣地	**more** angrily 較生氣地	**most** angrily 最生氣地
quickly 快地	**more** quickly 較快地	**most** quickly 最快地

(c) 有些副詞比較級和最高級的構成屬於不規則變化。

原　級	比　較　級	最　高　級
badly 壞地	worse 較壞地	worst 最壞地
well 很好地	better 較好地	best 最好地
late 遲、晚	later 較遲地	latest/last 最遲地／最後地
little 少、幾乎不	less 較少、較不	least 最少、最不
much 很	more 較	most 最

小練習

請寫出下列副詞的比較級和最高級。

1. far ＿＿＿＿＿＿＿ ＿＿＿＿＿＿＿
2. easily ＿＿＿＿＿＿＿ ＿＿＿＿＿＿＿
3. little ＿＿＿＿＿＿＿ ＿＿＿＿＿＿＿
4. tastefully ＿＿＿＿＿＿＿ ＿＿＿＿＿＿＿
5. softly ＿＿＿＿＿＿＿ ＿＿＿＿＿＿＿
6. tearfully ＿＿＿＿＿＿＿ ＿＿＿＿＿＿＿
7. excitedly ＿＿＿＿＿＿＿ ＿＿＿＿＿＿＿
8. gleefully ＿＿＿＿＿＿＿ ＿＿＿＿＿＿＿
9. visibly ＿＿＿＿＿＿＿ ＿＿＿＿＿＿＿
10. profusely ＿＿＿＿＿＿＿ ＿＿＿＿＿＿＿
11. neatly ＿＿＿＿＿＿＿ ＿＿＿＿＿＿＿
12. attentively ＿＿＿＿＿＿＿ ＿＿＿＿＿＿＿
13. dangerously ＿＿＿＿＿＿＿ ＿＿＿＿＿＿＿
14. disgracefully ＿＿＿＿＿＿＿ ＿＿＿＿＿＿＿
15. strangely ＿＿＿＿＿＿＿ ＿＿＿＿＿＿＿
16. early ＿＿＿＿＿＿＿ ＿＿＿＿＿＿＿
17. late ＿＿＿＿＿＿＿ ＿＿＿＿＿＿＿
18. cleverly ＿＿＿＿＿＿＿ ＿＿＿＿＿＿＿
19. dirtily ＿＿＿＿＿＿＿ ＿＿＿＿＿＿＿
20. straight ＿＿＿＿＿＿＿ ＿＿＿＿＿＿＿
21. bitterly ＿＿＿＿＿＿＿ ＿＿＿＿＿＿＿
22. purposely ＿＿＿＿＿＿＿ ＿＿＿＿＿＿＿
23. simply ＿＿＿＿＿＿＿ ＿＿＿＿＿＿＿
24. permanently ＿＿＿＿＿＿＿ ＿＿＿＿＿＿＿
25. happily ＿＿＿＿＿＿＿ ＿＿＿＿＿＿＿
26. much ＿＿＿＿＿＿＿ ＿＿＿＿＿＿＿

27. highly _____ _____　28. fast _____

29. badly _____ _____　30. well _____

31. loudly _____ _____　32. near _____

☞ 更多相關習題請見本章應用練習 Part 1～Part 2。

9-3 比較的句型

(a) 當兩個同等的人或事物相互比較時，主要可用兩個句型："...as + Adj./Adv. + as..."、"...not + as/so + Adj./Adv. + as..."。

USAGE PRACTICE

形容詞

▶ He looks as **red** as a beet. 他的臉像甜菜根一樣紅。

▶ He is as **brave** as a lion. 他像獅子一樣勇敢。

▶ He is as **strong** as a bull. 他像公牛一樣強壯。

▶ I am not as **clever** as my cousin. 我不像我表姐那麼聰明。

▶ I am just as **fast** as she is. 我像她一樣快。

▶ He is not so **strong** as Hercules. 他不像海格力斯那麼強壯。

▶ No other person is so **mischievous** as you. 沒有其他人像你一樣頑皮。

▶ This pencil is not as **sharp** as that one. 這支鉛筆不像那支那樣尖。

▶ Your watch is not as **expensive** as mine. 你的手錶不像我的那麼昂貴。

▶ You are not so **foolish** as I thought. 你不像我想的那樣笨。

▶ I'm not so **stupid** as you think. 我不像你想得那樣愚蠢。

▶ They are not so **intelligent** as you may think. 他們不像你想的那麼聰明。

▶ The service here is not so **satisfactory** as in that shop.
　這裡的服務不像那一家店的那麼令人滿意。

副詞

▶ She dresses as **fashionably** as you do. 她穿得和你一樣時髦。

▶ I came as **early** as I could. 我儘早來了。

▶ We can do this as **well** as you. 我們能把這件事做得和你一樣好。

▶ Maria can read as **fast** as you. 瑪莉亞能像你讀得一樣快。

▶ She dances as **gracefully** as her sister. 她跳舞和她姊姊一樣優雅。

(b) 當兩個不同等的人或事物相互比較時，主要都是用「比較級 + than」的句型來表達。

USAGE PRACTICE

形容詞

▶ She is **older** than I am. 她比我年長。

▶ My essay is **worse** than yours. 我的論文比你的差。

▶ My book is **thicker** than yours. 我的書比你的厚。

▶ He is **younger** than all of them. 他比他們所有的人都年輕。

▶ John does **more** work than all of us put together.

約翰做的工作比我們所有人做的加起來還要多。

▶ This house is **more beautiful** than that one. 這間房子比那間漂亮。

▶ My work is certainly **better** than yours. 我的工作確實比你的好。

▶ His writing is **worse** than his sister's. 他的書寫比他妹妹的還糟。

▶ Purple is a **more interesting** color than red. 紫色是比紅色更有趣的顏色。

▶ The necklace is **more valuable** than the bracelet. 這條項鍊要比這個手鐲更有價值。

副詞

▶ Edward writes **more carefully** than you. 愛德華寫得比你更加仔細小心。

▶ He paints **more beautifully** than she does. 他畫得比她畫得更漂亮。

▶ He works **harder** than all of you. 他比你們所有人更努力工作。

▶ This boy did his work **faster** than that one did. 這個男孩工作要比那個男孩速度快。

▶ He can run **faster** than all these boys. 他能夠跑得比所有這些男孩快。

▶ He has stayed here **longer** than you have. 他停留在這裡的時間比你久。

▶ He drives the car much **faster** than his father. 他開這輛車比他父親開得快很多。

▶ She finished her work **more quickly** than we did. 她比我們更快地把工作完成。

▶ He behaved even **more rudely** than I had expected. 他的行為比我預期的還要更粗魯。

▶ They behaved **more kindly** toward her than we did. 他們對她的舉止比我們對她更親切。

---

 less 也是比較級的用法，不過表達的是「較少」的意思。如果用在形容詞或副詞前面，就會形成否定的比較級。

▶ You put in **less** effort than Thomas. 你比湯瑪斯還不努力。

▶ I have **less** money than you have. 我的錢比你的錢少。

基礎文法寶典 ❷
Essential English Usage & Grammar

▶ You spend **less** than that person. 你花的錢比那個人少。

▶ Henry does his work **less carefully** than Benny. 亨利工作比班尼更不仔細。

(c) 一般常用 other 來比較一個人或事物與其他相似的人或事物的差別。

USAGE PRACTICE

▶ Hercules was **stronger** than the other three men. 海格力斯比另外三個人更強壯。

▶ Tokyo has a **larger** population than all other cities in Japan.

東京的人口比日本所有其他城市多。

▶ Rio de Janeiro is **more beautiful** than all the other ports.

里約熱內盧比所有其它港口美麗。

▶ Colin is **cleverer** than other boys. 科林比其他男孩聰明。

 此類比較級的句型可以代換成最高級的用法。

▶ Hercules was **the strongest** of all men. 海格力斯是所有人當中最強壯的。

▶ Tokyo has **the largest** population of all cities in Japan. 東京的人口是日本所有城市中最多的。

(d) 有時候，可以不用 than 來表示比較級的意味。

USAGE PRACTICE

▶ She wants to buy a **bigger** refrigerator for her kitchen.

她想要為她的廚房添購一個更大的冰箱。

▶ Is she your **younger** sister? 她是你的妹妹嗎？

▶ His **elder** brother is the owner of the shop. 他的哥哥是這家商店的店主。

▶ His condition is **worse** today. 他今天的狀況比較糟。

▶ The people must be evacuated before the water rises **higher**.

這些人們必須在水漲得更高之前撤離。

▶ I want a **larger** piece of paper. 我想要一張更大的紙。

▶ The teacher wants the work written **more neatly**. 老師想要作業被寫得更整齊。

▶ You must climb **higher** if you wish to have a better view.

如果你想看到更好的景色，你必須爬得更高。

▶ He is waiting till the fruit is **riper**. 他在等待水果更熟點。

(e) 當三個以上的人或事物做比較時，要用最高級的句型。由於比較時往往會有範圍，所以常會加上介系詞片語或子句來界定。

USAGE PRACTICE

▶ This is **the lightest** of the three parcels. 這是三個包裹當中最輕的一個。

▶ I had **the biggest** shock of my life. 我遇到我一生中最大的打擊。

▶ It was **the most frightening** incident of my life. 這是我一生當中發生最可怕的事件。

▶ Mt. Everest is **the highest** mountain in the world. 埃佛勒斯峰是世界上最高的山。

▶ He is **the cleverest** boy in the class. 他是這一班最聰明的男生。

▶ This is **the best** that I can do. 這是我能做到最好的了。

▶ She dressed **the most beautifully** of all the girls. 在所有的女孩當中，她是最精心打扮的。

▶ This is **the easiest** problem I have ever solved. 這是我曾經解決過最容易的問題。

▶ He is **the worst** player in the team. 他是這一隊裡最差的球員。

▶ He has **the worst** temper in the office. 在這個辦公室裡，他的脾氣最差。

▶ That team scored **the most** points in the match. 那個隊伍在比賽中得到最多的分數。

▶ Of the three girls, Marie bakes **the most delicious** cakes.
  在這三個女孩中，瑪麗烘焙的蛋糕最美味。

(f) 最高級通常要加上定冠詞 the，但是不做直接比較時，可以省略 the 或使用不定冠詞 a。此時，most 表示「非常、很」。

USAGE PRACTICE

▶ Marie's cakes are **most delicious**. 瑪麗做的蛋糕是非常美味的。

▶ Lily is wearing a **most beautiful** dress. 莉莉正穿著一件非常漂亮的洋裝。

▶ That was a **most beautiful** piece of work. 那是一件非常美麗的作品。

▶ It was raining **most heavily** on my return journey. 在我的回程中雨下得非常大。

▶ That was a **most boring** talk. 那是一場非常無聊的演說。

▶ She is a **most charming** person. 她是個很有魅力的人。

▶ We have just received a **most interesting** letter from her.
  我們剛收到她寄來一封非常有趣的信。

▶ She wrote a **most lengthy** essay. 她寫了一篇很長的論文。

> He had a **most brilliant** idea. 他有一個很棒的主意。

(g) 在同一個句子中，若出現兩個比較級或最高級，較短的字應該置於較長的之前。

USAGE PRACTICE

> He is the **smaller** but **stronger** of the two boys.

他是這兩個男孩中個子比較小但比較強壯的。

> He is **older** and **more experienced** than you. 他比你年長且比較有經驗。

> He is the **youngest** but the **most intelligent** of the boys.

他是這些男孩中最年輕，但也是最聰明的。

(h) 比較級和最高級可以使用於一些慣用法的句型中。

USAGE PRACTICE

> The **more**, the **merrier**. 多多益善。

> If the **worst** comes to the **worst**, I can always walk home.

如果最壞的情形發生了，我還能走回家。

> He seemed to grow **taller** and **taller**. 他好像長得越來越高。

> Her cold is getting **worse** and **worse**. 她的感冒愈來愈嚴重。

小練習

請選擇正確的形容詞或副詞形式填入空格中。

1. He got _____ (*best; better*) marks this term although the tests were _____ (*harder, hardest*) than those of last term.

2. Although we were as _____ (*hungry; hungrier*) as bears, we did not eat as _____ (*much; more*) as we usually do.

3. Which can run _____ (*fastest; faster*)—a horse or a donkey?

4. This is the _____ _____ (*more popular; most popular*) song on the radio at the moment.

5. Will you be _____ _____ (*most careful; more careful*) about what you say in the future? In fact, the _____ (*least; less*) you speak, the _____ (*good; better*) it will be for all of us!

6. If you had _____ (*much; more*) money, do you think you would be any _____ (*happiest; happier*)?

7. If you take a taxi, you will arrive _____ (*earlier; earliest*) than all of us. We don't want to be the _____ (*earlier; earliest*), so we'll take the bus.

8. Tin is the _____ _____ (*more important; most important*) mineral in the country. The next _____ _____ (*more important; most important*) minerals are iron and gold.

9. The central part of Moonglade is the _____ _____ (*less developed; least developed*) part of the island because the swamps are _____ (*wider; widest*) there.

10. He does the _____ (*more; most*) business during the school holidays. This is usually the _____ (*busier; busiest*) time of the year for him.

11. His handwriting is getting _____ (*badly; worse*) and _____ (*worst; worse*) every year. My eyesight is not any _____ (*good; better*) after reading his work.

12. He will become _____ (*angriest; angrier*) if you don't tell him the truth. Moreover, you will feel _____ (*good; better*) after you have confided in him.

☞ 更多相關習題請見本章應用練習 Part 3～Part 11。

9-4 較進階的比較級用法

(a) far 有兩種比較級和最高級。一般而言，表示「距離」時，用 farther、farthest；而在其他情形中，尤其是表示「程度」時，用 further、furthest。

USAGE PRACTICE

▶ Peter jumped **farther** than anybody else in the competition.

　彼得比競賽中的任何其他人都跳得遠。

▶ He threw the discus **farther** than I did.　他擲鐵餅擲得比我遠。

▶ I walked **farther** than anyone else today.　今天我走得比其他任何人都遠。

▶ She threw her books into the **farthest** corner of the hall, in a sudden outburst of temper.

　在一陣勃然大怒之下，她把她的書丟到大廳最遠的角落。

▶ Who ran the **farthest** in the race?　誰在比賽中跑得最遠？

▶ I will send you **further** details tomorrow.　明天我會把更進一步的細節寄給你。

▶ Do you have anything **further** to add?　你有進一步的東西要補充的嗎？

▶ Murder was **furthest** from his mind when he committed the robbery.

當犯下搶案時，他從未想到過要殺人。

(b) old 也有兩種比較級和最高級。older 和 oldest 用來表示「年齡大小」，elder 和 eldest 則用來表示「一個家庭中成員的輩份大小或長幼次序」。

USAGE PRACTICE

▶ Tom is **older** than Peter. 湯姆比彼得年紀大。

▶ Her sister is **older** than all the other girls in the class. 她姊姊的年紀比班上其他女孩大。

▶ Kenny is two years **older** than his brother. 肯尼比他的弟弟大兩歲。

▶ She is the **oldest** member of the society. 她是這個社群中年紀最大的成員。

▶ He is the **oldest** boy in my class. 他是我班上年紀最大的男生。

▶ The **oldest** in a group is not always the leader. 團體中年齡最大的並不一定總是領導者。

▶ I am his **elder** brother. 我是他的哥哥。

▶ Both my **elder** sisters are married. 我兩個姊姊都結婚了。

▶ My **elder** brother accompanied me to the station. 我哥哥陪我去車站。

▶ John is the **eldest** in his family. 約翰是他家裡輩分最高的。

▶ His **eldest** brother is here to see you. 他的大哥來這裡看你了。

▶ The **eldest** in the family bears a heavy load of responsibility.
家中輩分最長者背負很重的責任。

 不過，現在的使用趨勢是 elder/eldest 僅用在表示哥哥、姊姊等少數情況，大部分其他情況都一律使用 older/oldest。此外，elder 後面也不可以接 than 來形成比較，只能接名詞。

▶ Jerry is 5 years **older** than me. 傑瑞比我大五歲。(×elder)

(c) senior、junior、superior、inferior、prior 或 preferable 等形容詞在比較級用法中後接介系詞 to，而不是 than。

USAGE PRACTICE

▶ He is **senior** to me in the office. 在辦公室裡他比我資深。

▶ This painting is **superior** to that one. 這幅畫比那一幅好。

▶ You are **superior** to her in experience. 你比她有經驗。

▶ All of these students are **junior** to us. 所有這些學生都比我年輕。

▶ He is **junior** to Peter in rank. 他的排行比彼得小。

▶ This piece of cloth is certainly **inferior** to that one. 這塊布料的確比那塊差。

▶ I have found a method **preferable** to that of any other person.

我已經找到一個方法，比其他任何人的方法都還要更好。

(d) late 也有兩種比較級和最高級。later、latest 指「時間早晚」，而另外一種比較級 latter 指「（兩者中的）後者」，最高級 last 指「（三者以上中的）最後一個」。

USAGE PRACTICE

▶ She arrived **later** than I did. 她比我晚到。

▶ You can come at a **later** time if you want. 如果你想，你可以晚點來。

▶ This is the **latest** fashion from Paris. 這是來自巴黎的最新流行的式樣。

▶ His **latest** book is a best-seller. 他最新的書很暢銷。

▶ Both Mary and Susan are coming but I want to talk only to the **latter**.

瑪麗和蘇珊都要來，但是我只想跟後者說話。（即蘇珊）

▶ She offered me margarine and butter. I chose the **latter**.

她給我人造奶油和奶油。我選了後者。（即奶油）

▶ Of the three—tea, milk and coffee—I prefer the **last**.

這三樣東西——茶、牛奶和咖啡——我喜歡最後一樣。

▶ Mary was the **last** to arrive at school. 瑪麗是最後一個到學校的。

(e) 以下兩個比較級的用法必須特別注意。less 用來指「較難精確計算的數量」，常與不可數名詞連用；而 fewer 指「可詳細點算的數目」，常與可數名詞連用。

USAGE PRACTICE

▶ There are **fewer** people here than I thought. 這裡的人比我以為的少。

▶ No **fewer** than three persons died in the collision. 在此次相撞事件中，不只三人死亡。

▶ She bought **less** than a kilogram of tea. 她買了不到一公斤的茶。

▶ I ate **less** than I normally do. 我比平常吃得還少。

▶ **Less** manual labor is used in mechanized industries. 較少的勞力被用在機械化的工業界。

請依照句子情境，將提示字以比較級或最高級的形式填入空格中。

1. Sally and Sandra are twin sisters; the _____ (late) is the _____ (old).

2. I am _____ (old) than my friend though we are both in the same class.

3. We walked _____ (far) into the woods, hoping to catch some more butterflies.

4. The _____ (few) people there are in the house, the _____ (little) trouble you'll have.

5. Don't you think that this film is _____ (good) than the _____ (late) one shown here?

6. If you have nothing _____ (far) to discuss, we will adjourn the meeting.

7. "Four kilometers is the _____ (far) that I can walk in an hour," the woman said.

8. The _____ (old) boy in my class is Oscar. He is seventeen years old and is the _____ (old) child in his family.

9. Give him one _____ (late) chance. If he fails this time, we can do nothing _____ (far) to help him.

10. We can travel either by sea or by air. Although the _____ (late) is the _____ (fast) of the two ways, we still prefer the former.

11. "Being the _____ (old) in the family is much _____ (good) than being the _____ (young)," she said.

12. This is the _____ (late) machine that can work _____ (efficiently) than an old one.

13. My _____ (near) neighbor is only a quarter of a kilometer away. When I have no _____ (far) chores to do, I always go to visit her.

14. That actress' _____ (late) film is a box-office draw. No _____ (few) than twenty of my friends have seen it.

15. The teacher praised her work for she had the _____ (few) mistakes in the _____ (late) test paper.

16. I have three sisters. My _____ (old) sister is about three years _____ (old) than I am. My brother is the _____ (young) in the family.

17. The _____ (late) day of the examinations is Thursday. After that we'll have no _____ (far) worries about examinations.

18. He is the _____ (old) boy in the family, and he is the _____ (clever) one, too.

19. The _____ (far) she can go in that old car is a kilometer or two. The _____ (little) you can do is to tell her about it.

20. My _____ (*old*) brother is four years _____ (*old*) than I am, but he is not the _____ (*old*) in the family.

21. I'm too tired to go any _____ (*far*).

22. John's _____ (*old*) brother is four years _____ (*old*) than he is.

23. My _____ (*old*) brother is two years _____ (*old*) than I am. I am _____ (*young*) than he is.

24. John is thirteen; Peter is fourteen; and Paul is fifteen. John is the _____ (*young*), and Paul is the _____ (*old*). Peter is _____ (*old*) than John, but not as old as Paul.

25. My friend has three brothers, the _____ (*old*) of whom is not even _____ (*old*) than the _____ (*old*) of my two brothers.

26. I arrived _____ (*late*) than usual because I had had a slight accident _____ (*far*) down the road. My _____ (*old*) brother, who was with me, helped me pick up the things that I had dropped from my bicycle.

Chapter 9　應用練習

PART 1

請寫出下列形容詞或副詞的比較級和最高級。

1. lovingly _____ _____　　2. sly _____ _____

3. plainly _____ _____　　4. fearful _____ _____

5. misleading _____ _____　　6. attractively _____ _____

7. sturdy _____ _____　　8. craftily _____ _____

9. puny _____ _____　　10. strongly _____ _____

11. few _____ _____　　12. merrily _____ _____

13. evil _____ _____　　14. amazing _____ _____

15. splendidly _____ _____　　16. feeble _____ _____

17. harsh _____ _____　　18. apt _____ _____

19. cheeky _____ _____　　20. frightfully _____ _____

21. renowned _____ _____　　22. stern _____ _____

23. speedily _____ _____　　24. marvelous _____ _____

25. thankfully _____ _____　　26. dependable _____ _____

27. courageous _____ _____ 28. glad _____ _____

PART 2

請寫出下列形容詞或副詞的比較級和最高級。

1. simple _____ _____   2. fine _____ _____

3. sadly _____ _____   4. gray _____ _____

5. barren _____ _____   6. commonly _____ _____

7. pleasantly _____ _____   8. quiet _____ _____

9. handsome _____ _____   10. polite _____ _____

11. many _____ _____   12. old _____ _____

13. able _____ _____   14. rapidly _____ _____

15. common _____ _____   16. miserable _____ _____

17. pleasant _____ _____   18. moody _____ _____

19. narrow _____ _____   20. extravagant _____ _____

21. swiftly _____ _____   22. fast _____ _____

23. soon _____ _____   24. immense _____ _____

25. thin _____ _____   26. big _____ _____

27. cheerfully _____ _____   28. superior _____ _____

PART 3

請依照句子情境，將提示字以原級、比較級或最高級的形式填入空格中。

1. There are only two ways to the market. Which is the _____ (*short*) way?

2. We usually eat _____ (*much*) than he does, but he eats _____ (*often*) than we do.

3. He is the _____ (*experienced*) teacher in the school since he has been there for twenty years.

4. He has always had the _____ (*good*) of everything.

5. It is raining _____ (*heavily*) now than it did last night.

6. A tiger is not as _____ (*large*) as an elephant. The mouse is probably the _____ (*small*) of all four-footed mammals.

7. He is the _____ (*accurate*) and can work _____ (*fast*) than all the

other workers in the firm.

8. English is an _____ (*easy*) language to learn than Chinese, while Russian is said to be the _____ (*difficult*) language of all.

9. I weigh 40 kilograms, John weighs 55 kilograms, and Andy weighs 65 kilograms. I am _____ (*light*) than John. John is _____ (*little*) heavy than Andy. Andy is the _____ (*heavy*).

10. He is much _____ (*fat*) than I am, so he is not so _____ (*healthy*) as I am.

11. The harvest this year is the _____ (*bad*) one since the war. If we don't get a _____ (*good*) harvest next year, we will have _____ (*little*) money to spend.

12. Of the three sisters, she is the _____ (*old*) and also the _____ (*pretty*).

13. The rich man wants to make a will as his health is getting _____ (*bad*) and _____ (*bad*) every day.

14. He can throw the discus _____ (*far*) than all of us, and yet he is the _____ (*bad*) runner in the whole class.

15. _____ (*many*) and _____ (*many*) people join the army every year.

PART 4

請依照句子情境，將提示字以原級、比較級或最高級的形式填入空格中。

1. She is the _____ (*kind*) woman that I have ever met.

2. A donkey is not so _____ (*intelligent*) as a horse.

3. This painting is _____ (*good*) than your last one. You are sure to get the _____ (*good*) price for it.

4. Which of the two photographs shows a _____ (*clear*) view of the building?

5. If he wants to pass his driving test, he has to drive _____ (*carefully*) and know the road signs _____ (*well*).

6. The neighbor's grass is always _____ (*green*).

7. Gary arrived _____ (*early*), but Kenneth had arrived even _____ (*early*). However, neither of them was as _____ (*early*) as Nelson.

8. You can get there quite _____ (*cheaply*) by car, _____ (*cheaply*) by

bus, and the _____ (*cheaply*) on foot.

9. She is not singing as _____ (*well*) as she did last year. Her voice is getting
_____ (*bad*) and _____ (*bad*).

10. He is feeling _____ (*little*) and _____ (*little*) comfortable in the hall.

11. Of the four countries, that one is the _____ (*advanced*); and the standard of
literacy there is the _____ (*high*).

12. John is the _____ (*clever*) of the two brothers.

PART 5

請依照句子情境，將提示字以原級、比較級或最高級的形式填入空格中。

1. This is the _____ (*high*) mountain in the country.

2. That one is _____ (*expensive*) than this one here.

3. It is _____ (*dangerous*) to drive along that road on a rainy day.

4. A car can go _____ (*fast*) than a bicycle, but an airplane can go the
_____ (*fast*).

5. Ford Street is the _____ (*good*) road to take when you are in a hurry.

6. Mr. Taylor is one of the _____ (*rich*) men in the town.

7. Today's weather is _____ (*hot*) than yesterday's.

8. A prize is given to the _____ (*cute*) baby in the show.

9. Which is the _____ (*strong*) of the two men?

10. All the dancers were _____ (*beautiful*), but the one in the center was
_____ (*beautiful*) than the rest.

11. That is not the _____ (*high*) building. There is one _____ (*tall*) than
that one.

12. Gary can draw _____ (*well*) than any of us, but his brother can draw the
_____ (*beautifully*).

13. This is the _____ (*thick*) piece of rope I can find. There isn't any other one
_____ (*thick*) than this in the house.

14. You can hear their voices _____ (*distinctly*) from here. However, if you step
_____ (*far*) away, they will become _____ (*little*) distinct.

15. Of the three boys, the _____ (*young*) one is the _____ (*cheeky*).

16. If he comes home _____ (*late*) than ten p.m., he will be locked out.

17. I am the _____ (*old*) in the family, so I have _____ (*great*) responsibility than any of my brothers or sisters.

18. The river here is _____ (*deep*) than anywhere else, so it is _____ (*difficult*) to swim across.

19. He ran as _____ (*fast*) as he could, but his pursuer was getting _____ (*near*) and _____ (*near*) to him.

20. My bird can sing _____ (*sweetly*) than yours, though yours is _____ (*pretty*).

PART 6

請依照句子情境，將提示字以原級、比較級或最高級的形式填入空格中。

1. The _____ (*much*) I can do for you is to lend you some money.

2. I've never met such a person. The _____ (*much*) you give him, the _____ (*little*) contented he is!

3. For _____ (*far*) information, you can buy a guidebook.

4. That is the _____ (*bad*) thing that has ever happened to me.

5. The _____ (*long*) he stays here, the _____ (*dangerous*) his position is.

6. At an auction, the _____ (*high*) bidder gets the article.

7. The _____ (*expensive*) thing is not necessarily the _____ (*valuable*).

8. It will be _____ (*bad*) for us if we run away.

9. You will soon be _____ (*well*) if you continue taking the medicine.

10. After a few weeks of rest, she looks _____ (*strong*) and _____ (*healthy*).

11. After a few exercises, you will find them _____ (*easy*) to do.

12. The _____ (*sharp*) of the two pencils is mine.

13. When Doug came back from his holiday, he looked _____ (*dark*) and _____ (*cheerful*).

14. I reminded myself to get up _____ (*early*) the next day in order to have time to prepare breakfast.

15. Put the _____ (*thick*) end of the pole into the ground so that it will stand upright.

16. After the accident, he was _____ (*careful*) about driving.

17. The diamond was sparkling _____ (*brightly*) as she moved her hand up and down.

18. As time passed, he grew _____ (*old*) and _____ (*wise*); _____ (*many*) people came to him for advice.

19. The illness was making her _____ (*weak*) each day, for it became _____ (*bad*) and _____ (*bad*).

20. As the hunters killed _____ (*many*) bisons, they became _____ (*few*) in number each day.

PART 7

請依照句子情境，將提示字以原級、比較級或最高級的形式填入空格中。

1. Can't you find a _____ (*good*) reason for your absence than that?

2. An apple is as _____ (*big*) as an orange, but it is _____ (*small*) than a watermelon.

3. It is _____ (*hot*) today than it was yesterday, but it is not as _____ (*hot*) as it was on Friday.

4. I ate _____ (*much*) than you did even though you were _____ (*hungry*) than I was.

5. Eddie has _____ (*many*) marbles than I have. I have _____ (*few*) than he has.

6. The _____ (*much*) time I spend on my work, the _____ (*little*) time I have for games.

7. She sings much _____ (*sweetly*) than the rest of us. She is the _____ (*good*) singer in our class.

8. The _____ (*careful*) you are when you are on the road, the _____ (*safe*) you will be.

9. He may be _____ (*strong*) than we are, but at least we are not as _____ (*rough*) as he is. We are _____ (*gentle*) than he is.

10. She said that it rained _____ (*heavily*) last night than the day before. I didn't know because I was sleeping _____ (*soundly*) than I usually do.

11. Both of them are intelligent. But the _____ (*old*) boy is _____ (*little*)

intelligent than the _____ (*young*) one.

12. This is the _____ (*good*) car in the whole workshop. It is the _____ (*cheap*), the _____ (*dangerous*), and the _____ (*economical*) car here.

13. Mary has seven apples. Sally has five. Alice has only three. Mary has the _____ (*many*), while Alice has the _____ (*few*). Sally doesn't have as _____ (*many*) as Mary, but _____ (*many*) than Alice.

PART 8

請依照句子情境，將提示字以原級、比較級或最高級的形式填入空格中。

1. He told us that goods nowadays should be _____ (*cheap*) since they are produced at a _____ (*fast*) rate.

2. Of the two boys, the _____ (*young*) boy is _____ (*intelligent*) and _____ (*hardworking*) than the other.

3. Mary is not as _____ (*heavy*) as Sally, but is certainly _____ (*clumsy*) than Sally.

4. That is the _____ (*beautiful*) boat I have ever seen. It is also the _____ (*speedy*) boat in the harbor.

5. Sometimes you can get _____ (*good*) things at a _____ (*cheap*) price.

6. He talks _____ (*much*) than he works. That is why he can't finish his work as _____ (*quickly*) as we can.

7. The floods will become even _____ (*bad*) if the rain pours _____ (*heavily*) than it does now.

8. You would have had _____ (*good*) results than this if you had worked _____ (*hard*) than you did.

9. This is one of the _____ (*interesting*) books I've read. Do you have any other books as _____ (*interesting*) as this one?

10. Last night was one of the _____ (*cold*) nights ever. I used _____ (*many*) blankets than I usually do and slept even _____ (*soundly*) than usual.

11. This is the _____ (*good*) news I've had for a long time. It is even _____ (*good*) than the news about my success in the examination.

12. She gets up _____ (*early*) than the rest of us and goes to bed _____

(*late*), too. But still she manages to look as _____ (*fresh*) as we do.

13. The _____ (*old*) sister is _____ (*pretty*) than the _____ (*young*) one, but the _____ (*young*) sister is _____ (*intelligent*) than the other.

14. She took the _____ (*little*) time to finish the work. We were much _____ (*slow*) than she was. Peter took the _____ (*much*) time since he had started _____ (*late*) than the rest of us.

PART 9

請依照句子情境，將提示字以比較級或最高級的形式填入空格中。

1. The police are conducting _____ (*far*) investigations to find the _____ (*late*) customer who left the jewelry shop.

2. This pot has the _____ (*little*) coffee in it.

3. The _____ (*far*) you run, the _____ (*tired*) you become. Then, you may have no _____ (*much*) energy to go home.

4. Our concert was _____ (*successful*) than we had expected. The audience, which numbered no _____ (*few*) than a thousand, applauded all the acts, especially the _____ (*late*) one.

5. Richard and Ronnie are brothers; the _____ (*late*) is the _____ (*old*) one.

6. The boys walked _____ (*far*) into the forest where the trees grew _____ (*thickly*) than in other parts. They walked very fast, with the _____ (*old*) among them being the _____ (*late*).

7. The hospital in the city has the _____ (*late*) medical equipment and is run _____ (*efficiently*) than the village hospital.

8. Of the three boys, his writing is the _____ (*bad*). It is strange that the _____ (*hard*) he tries to improve it, the _____ (*bad*) it becomes.

9. The _____ (little) you talk, the _____ (*far*) you'll jump and the _____ (*likely*) you'll be to win a prize.

10. The teacher placed her in the _____ (*far*) seat in the class because she is the _____ (*talkative*) of the girls.

11. Of all the girls, Kathy arrived the _____ (*late*). She said that she lived the _____ (*far*) away from the school.

12. The _____ (*little*) that you can do is to help us carry these new books to the library which is at the _____ (*far*) end of the school.

13. Of these two witnesses, the _____ (*late*) seemed _____ (*afraid*) and _____ (*hesitant*).

14. It is _____ (*unfortunate*) that we could not buy tickets for this show. We will have to see a _____ (*late*) show and hope that there will be no _____ (*far*) delay in buying the tickets.

PART 10

請依照句子情境，將提示字以原級、比較級或最高級的形式填入空格中。

1. Even though he has _____ (*few*) classes to teach, he seems to have _____ (*little*) time than you.

2. No other boy is as _____ (*studious*) as Henry. He spends _____ (*much*) time in the library than at the playground.

3. He is the _____ (*young*) but the _____ (*intelligent*) boy in the class. He always scores the _____ (*high*) marks in all examinations.

4. Tracy's painting is _____ (*good*) and _____ (*expressive*) than her sister's.

5. The _____ (*much*) he thought about it, the _____ (*angry*) he became.

6. She is _____ (*clever*) and _____ (*beautiful*) by far, but she has the _____ (*bad*) temper, too.

7. He is not so _____ (*obstinate*) as his _____ (*young*) brother and is far _____ (*friendly*) than he is.

8. We should choose the _____ (*simple*) and the _____ (*effective*) method to deal with a problem.

9. She had filled in the form as _____ (*well*) as she could, but still the clerk asked her for _____ (*many*) details.

10. The _____ (*much*) I work, the _____ (*little*) I seem to accomplish; I'm getting _____ (*desperate*) as the deadline draws _____ (*near*).

11. The _____ (*long*) you work, the _____ (*much*) you will earn and the _____ (*secure*) you will be.

12. He was _____ (*pleased*) than anybody else to hear the results.

13. The Nile is said to be one of the _____ (*long*) rivers and the Amazon one of the _____ (*large*).

14. I had a _____ (*frightful*) experience as I was walking home one night. The darkness had never seemed _____ (*unfriendly*) or the silence _____ (*terrifying*).

15. She has the _____ (*light*) and the _____ (*soothing*) touch of all the nurses here.

16. This parade of the stars is certainly the _____ (*lively*), the _____ (*colorful*), and the _____ (*spectacular*) event of the year.

17. Her parents are _____ (*worried*) about her education than she herself is. They are constantly enquiring whether she is doing any _____ (*good*) or _____ (*bad*) in class.

18. The cover of this book is not as _____ (*impressive*) as the cover of that one, but the former book is _____ (*interesting*). It is borrowed _____ (*frequently*) than the latter.

19. The water is _____ (*deep*) and the current _____ (*strong*) where the bank curves sharply. It is _____ (*dangerous*) to swim across there, too.

PART 11

請依照句子情境，將提示字以原級、比較級或最高級的形式填入空格中。

1. This design is not very beautiful. I'd like to see a _____ (*beautiful*) one.

2. The _____ (*fast*) we work, the _____ (*soon*) we'll finish this assignment.

3. Mr. Johnson gave a _____ (*interesting*) lecture to the Fifth Form students.

4. He has lost his job and is _____ (*bad*) off than ever.

5. As the wind became _____ (*strong*) and _____ (*strong*), we decided to stop the game.

6. Look! My kite is flying _____ (*high*) and _____ (*high*).

7. She is as _____ (*stubborn*) as her sister but not as _____ (*bad-tempered*).

8. If the _____ (*bad*) comes to the _____ (*bad*), we can always give our opponents a walkover.

9. You did _____ (*little*) than Anthony, but you feel _____ (*tired*) than he does.

10. That was a _____ (*impolite*) thing to say to a friend.

11. Stanley is the _____ (*well-mannered*) boy that I know. He is also the _____ (*helpful*) and the _____ (*hardworking*).

12. The _____ (*much*) I get to know you, the _____ (*little*) I understand you.

13. The _____ (*much*) you argue with that stubborn man, the _____ (*angry*) he'll get.

14. She considers him the _____ (*attractive*) person that she has ever met.

15. "Take it or leave it! This is the _____ (*low*) price that I can give you," the shopkeeper said.

16. As the water rose _____ (*high*) and _____ (*high*), the little boy climbed into a tub and managed to stay afloat. He was _____ (*resourceful*) than I had expected.

PART 12

請依照句子情境，將合適的用字填入空格中。

1. "He is the cleverest _____ my students," Mr. Young said.

2. He plays badminton better _____ his brother.

3. My work always seems to be much inferior _____ his.

4. It was _____ most awkward moment when she accused him of stealing her brooch.

5. This is quite expensive. If you want something _____ , you should find another brand.

6. He can draw a better picture _____ the rest of his classmates.

7. The situation is already bad enough; please do not make it any _____ .

8. My neighbor looks after his garden _____ carefully than I do.

9. He is the cleverest boy in the class. That is why he always gets _____ marks than anyone

146

else.

10. This watch is no good at all. I would like to buy a _____ one.

11. He is senior _____ me by two years, but he is _____ childish as my little brother.

12. I did the work _____ quickly _____ I could, but I still could not make it on time.

13. She has _____ clothes than you. Her wardrobe is more packed than yours.

14. Tom is my _____ brother. He is twenty years old. Next comes Susan, who is three years older _____ I am. I am the _____ in my family. Susan is _____ than Tom, but _____ than I am.

基礎文法寶典❷
Essential English Usage & Grammar

習題解答

Chapter 6 解答

6-1 小練習

1. in　2. with　3. about　4. on　5. from　6. to/about　7. with　8. for　9. at

10. with/at; about　11. at/for　12. with　13. for; with　14. with　15. with; with　16. in; for

6-4 小練習

1. from　2. at/with/about　3. at/with/about/over　4. on; in　5. of; at/by　6. at; of　7. with; of

8. for; of/at　9. to; with　10. in; with　11. at/by; with

6-6 小練習

1. for; of; among　2. of; in; for　3. of; in; of　4. through; with; of　5. under; for; against; for

6. for; of/on/about; in; of　7. from; in; of　8. for; in; for　9. with; to; on　10. on; of; for

11. in; in; for　12. on; of; from; to; to; on; about　13. from; on; among

應用練習

PART 1

1. off; out　2. at; at; at; to　3. at; for　4. by; out; at; of　5. at; for; for　6. at; up/along

7. at; of　8. for; in; by　9. for; at; on　10. for; in; of　11. about; on　12. to; in; of

13. on/to; with/in　14. along; for; from　15. in/into　16. through; from

PART 2

1. about　2. against; on　3. at; from　4. at/with; to　5. with/at/by; for　6. with; for

7. between; to/toward　8. from; by　9. with; for　10. for; for　11. on; in　12. on; to

13. of; with; from　14. about; of; on　15. between; on; in; in; from

PART 3

1. upon/into/on　2. on　3. from; to　4. with; on; out　5. with; for　6. on; to; in　7. of; to

8. on; for; from　9. At; from; to　10. to; for; in/of; in　11. of; by; in　12. of/into/to; in; on

13. over; on; with

PART 4

1. at　2. of; for　3. for; to/toward　4. with; at/with/about　5. of; about; for　6. of; from

7. to; for　8. for; of　9. of; of　10. with; in　11. on; about　12. at/by; of; of

PART 5

1. for; to　2. on; of　3. of; from　4. from; to　5. against; for; up; to　6. for; of; of

7. to; to; of　8. of; with; of　9. for; on; to　10. of; against; by　11. in; under; of

12. to/on/about; for; to   13. from; on; in; on   14. to; to/with; about; about   17. against; in; to; in; for

PART 6

1. to   2. to; by   3. from   4. in; by; on   5. to   6. at; in   7. at; by   8. for   9. from; in

10. at; on; from   11. under   12. in   13. on; for   14. to; in

PART 7

1. at; in   2. out of; without; from   3. with; to   4. in; up; in   5. on; out; on   6. in; near

7. up; from; onto   8. at; in   9. beside; in   10. along; from; to   11. on; at   12. from; by; into

PART 8

1. of; over; from   2. at; of; from   3. for; for   4. for; in   5. over; under; at; by   6. from; for; at

7. against   8. about; of   9. with; over/about; with   10. to/with; on; for   11. to   12. at; with

13. about; for   14. from

PART 9

1. in; for   2. in; out; of   3. about; to/into; of   4. in; in; to   5. for; with   6. to/on; in

7. from; by; through   8. with; in   9. of; from; in   10. on; from; for   11. at; to; at   12. of; with

13. in; of; at   14. in; by   15. on; to; to

PART 10

1. to; on   2. to; at; on   3. of; in   4. in; beside   5. into; in; for   6. into; into   7. to; by

8. of; to   9. of; to   10. with; on   11. to; on   12. from; for   13. on   14. at; for; to; to

PART 11

1. on; in   2. at; on; of   3. for; by   4. between; of; of   5. for; against   6. on; from

7. on; before   8. at; in; below   9. for; across   10. about; of; by   11. around; by   12. of; at

13. after; before/after   14. among; after; among   15. about; on; at

PART 12

1. without; since   2. up; to   3. to/into; through   4. out; of; to; over   5. since   6. into; into

7. to   8. into; past   9. within; without   10. without; with   11. to; through   12. over; under   13. to

14. with; to

PART 13

1. between; with   2. against; for   3. off; of   4. on; in   5. in; with   6. for   7. on; from

8. without   9. around; for   10. with/beside; for   11. up; under/near   12. into; at; in

13. by; in; of; of; of

PART 14

1. At　2. into　3. into　4. off; to　5. up　6. over　7. on; up　8. out　9. on/upon; of
10. in; out

PART 15

1. in; to　2. at/about; of　3. in; of　4. by; of　5. in; for　6. on; of　7. as; of　8. at; of
9. in; of　10. out; in; with　11. at; for　12. in; for　13. in; for　14. under; to　15. for　16. since

PART 16

1. since　2. for　3. for　4. since　5. for　6. for　7. since　8. since　9. for　10. for
11. since　12. since　13. for; since　14. for　15. since; for　16. for　17. for　18. since; Since
19. since　20. for　21. for　22. for　23. Since　24. since　25. For　26. for

PART 17

1. in　2. on　3. in　4. for　5. to　6. by　7. for　8. on　9. on/upon　10. on　11. of
12. off　13. of　14. off　15. with; off

PART 18

1. of; of　2. of; up　3. from　4. over　5. about　6. over　7. with　8. with　9. about; to
10. with　11. after　12. with; around　13. with　14. at; in; to; in　15. on; without; into

PART 19

1. with; at　2. to; by　3. from; up; to; at　4. through; down; to　5. on; at; near; with; at
6. on; of; on; of; down　7. Within; with; into; of　8. into; toward; of; toward　9. to; for; in; with; in
10. to; on; of; against; with　11. across; on; to; for; on; with; of　12. through/by; of; to; for; on; at

PART 20

1. at　2. from　3. with　4. at/with/about　5. with; at　6. about; for　7. with　8. for; of
9. with; to　10. at; of　11. with; in　12. on; of　13. about; for　14. of; of

PART 21

1. upon/on/at; about　2. from; into　3. for; for　4. after; over　5. to; between
6. around; behind　7. on; to　8. on; of　9. for; across　10. for; for　11. of/about　12. on; from
13. for; for　14. to/with; into　15. on; with; at

PART 22

1. for; from　2. of　3. for; at　4. at　5. between　6. for　7. of　8. of/over　9. to
10. on/about　11. in　12. in　13. from; for

PART 23

1. by　2. along　3. through　4. off　5. between　6. since　7. up　8. by　9. for　10. in

11. below   12. after   13. on   14. of   15. about   16. of   17. for   18. below

PART 24

1. with; to/with   2. from; after   3. up; in/into   4. up; for   5. to; for; from   6. off; at   7. at; on

8. with; on   9. from; in   10. on; in   11. at; at   12. to; for; of   13. into; by

Chapter 7 解答

7-1 小練習

1. hospitable   2. reluctant   3. inclusive   4. ritualistic   5. fanciful   6. lenient   7. irritable

8. hateful   9. legible   10. doubtful   11. impulsive   12. wrathful   13. wealthy   14. expensive

15. resourceful   16. stimulating   17. national   18. experienced   19. removable   20. original

21. critical   22. disobedient   23. risky   24. significant

7-3 小練習

1. her   2. their   3. my   4. my/our; yours   5. our; theirs   6. his; his   7. your; mine

8. yours; mine   9. its; its   10. our; theirs   11. Her   12. his; my   13. their; its; its   14. our; my; hers

15. your; her; yours

7-4 小練習

1. any; some   2. some; any   3. any; some   4. any; some   5. some; some   6. any; some

7. some/any; any   8. any; some   9. any; any   10. Some; some   11. Some; any   12. any; some

13. any; some

7-6 小練習

1. Sally is as old as I.   2. It will be easy enough for you to learn on your own.   3. Matthew had more video games than I.   4. The water is warm enough to swim.   5. The bread was too stale to be eaten.   6. Judy is the smartest student in this class.   7. The bag is so large that you can put all these things into it.   8. That book is more interesting than this one.   9. This book is too difficult for me to understand.   10. Jerry was so kind that everyone liked him very much.

應用練習

PART 1

1. feverish   2. complementary   3. stony   4. humorous   5. accidental   6. sensational

7. spicy   8. important   9. historical   10. comfortable   11. reliable   12. divisible

13. meddlesome   14. sorrowful   15. rectangular   16. pious   17. sanitary

PART 2

1. famous   2. triangular   3. snobbish   4. vigorous   5. hygienic   6. dangerous   7. scientific

8. chaotic   9. boyish   10. mischievous   11. attractive   12. furious   13. monstrous   14. acrobatic

15. habitual   16. foolish   17. cautious   18. insulting   19. progressive   20. solitary   21. persuasive

22. productive   23. energetic

PART 3

1. poisonous   2. influential   3. sympathetic   4. cowardly   5. atomic   6. Chinese

7. complimentary   8. numerous   9. honorable   10. economic   11. studious   12. democratic

13. spacious   14. armed

PART 4

1. central   2. criminal   3. fashionable   4. typical   5. possessive   6. obedient   7. gigantic

8. mysterious   9. excessive   10. hasty   11. personal   12. heroic   13. disastrous   14. muscular

15. memorable   16. envious   17. attentive   18. silent   19. hungry   20. deceitful   21. advisable

PART 5

1. illogical   2. irresolute   3. incompatible   4. incompetent   5. unreal   6. unused

7. irrelevant   8. unqualified   9. unquestioned   10. displeasing   11. insoluble   12. incombustible

13. dissatisfied   14. unthinkable   15. unscrupulous   16. untiring   17. dispassionate   18. dissimilar

19. inconstant   20. irremovable   21. disreputable   22. impotent   23. impracticable

PART 6

1. drowning   2. torn   3. annoying   4. increasing   5. excited   6. boring   7. amused

8. burning   9. closing   10. burned   11. absorbed   12. amusing; haunted   13. frightened

PART 7

1. (a) disappointing (b) disappointed   2. (a) insulted (b) insulting   3. (a) pleasing (b) pleased

4. (a) irritated (b) irritating   5. (a) boring (b) bored   6. (a) puzzling (b) puzzled

7. (a) exhausting (b) exhausted   8. (a) increasing (b) increased   9. (a) interesting (b) interested

10. (a) satisfying (b) satisfied   11. (a) amazed (b) amazing   12. (a) comforting (b) comforted

13. (a) shocking (b) shocked   14. (a) distinguished (b) distinguishing   15. (a) tiring (b) tired

16. (a) affected (b) affecting   17. (a) darkening (b) darkened   18. (a) fallen (b) falling

PART 8

1. friendly; religious   2. stealthy   3. innocent; intentional   4. Indian; remarkable

5. silvery; enchanting   6. neglected   7. original; raging   8. obedient; deliberate

9. sensational; dangerous   10. troublesome; difficult   11. European; spicy Asian

12. broken; blistered   13. progressive; fair   14. constructive; destructive   15. attractive; charming

16. impatient; steady   17. following; simplified   18. responsible; willing; exhausting; rewarding

PART 9

1. your; ours; his   2. their; my   3. her; hers; their   4. His; his; her   5. your; ours; our; our

6. my; my; your; Its   7. his; his; his; Her   8. our; her; hers   9. your; mine; my; my

10. Its; its; its; its   11. your; yours   12. my; mine; yours; mine; his   13. their; ours; their; theirs

14. his; yours; his; your   15. her; hers; Her; his   16. their; their; their; their

PART 10

1. our; Our   2. my; his   3. their; ours; ours   4. Our; our   5. their; his/her   6. his; his; hers

7. mine; its   8. your; theirs   9. their; ours   10. its   11. their; his   12. my; yours   13. his; hers

14. your; hers   15. Our; his/her; our   16. his; his   17. his; his; hers   18. its; our

PART 11

1. his; their   2. my; his   3. her; its   4. its   5. his; their   6. ours   7. their; their

8. your; yours   9. her; hers   10. my; its   11. their; mine   12. his; his   13. her; her; Her

14. our; theirs   15. our; his; His

PART 12

1. his; his; his   2. my; your; your   3. your; your; theirs   4. your; Mine   5. your; yours; theirs

6. ours; his   7. my; hers   8. my; our; her; mine   9. his; their; their   10. its   11. their

12. our; our   13. Your; mine; yours   14. our; our; ours   15. their   16. her; my   17. his; his

18. your; mine

PART 13

1. Some; any   2. some; any   3. Some; any   4. any   5. some   6. some; any   7. some; any

8. Some   9. some   10. some; any   11. some; any   12. any; some   13. some; any   14. some; any

15. some; any   16. some; some   17. some; any   18. any; some   19. some; any   20. some; any

21. some

PART 14

1. some; any   2. any   3. any; some   4. some   5. some; any   6. any   7. some; some

8. some; any   9. some; some   10. any   11. some; some   12. any; any   13. some; any

14. any; some   15. any; any   16. any; some   17. Some; some; any   18. some; any; some

19. any; some; some   20. any   21. any; some   22. some; some   23. some; some   24. some; any

PART 15

1. much; Many; a little   2. many; a few   3. much; much/a little   4. much; many/a few

5. a few; much   6. many; many/a few   7. many; many   8. a little; a few   9. a little; a little; a few

10. a little; a few   11. a few; much   12. a few/many; a little   13. many; a few; a little   14. a little

15. much; a few   16. much; a little

PART 16

1. a little; much   2. Much; a few   3. many; a little   4. much; a little   5. many; a few   6. a little

7. Much   8. a little   9. much   10. much; many   11. many; a few   12. much; many

13. many; much

Chapter 8 解答

8–1 小練習

1. gradually   2. cheaply   3. extremely   4. generously   5. probably   6. deliberately

7. regularly   8. boldly   9. terribly   10. lazily   11. rapidly   12. punctually   13. happily

14. thoughtfully   15. dramatically   16. slightly   17. cruelly   18. shamefully   19. heavily

20. specially   21. nobly   22. sleepily   23. noisily   24. beautifully   25. suddenly   26. bravely

27. practically   28. prettily   29. hungrily   30. miserably

8–3 小練習

1. patiently   2. accidentally   3. loudly   4. early   5. badly   6. generously   7. punctually

8. heavily   9. Gently; skillfully   10. regularly; fluently   11. politely   12. fiercely; nervously

13. safely   14. now; well   15. dearly

8–4 小練習

1. The team practiced hard on the school field all day.   2. I have been to Skyline Beach several times this month.   3. This area is under curfew daily for eight hours.   4. She missed her parents badly while they were abroad last month.   5. She sang beautifully in the contest last evening.   6. The baby was crying loudly in the next room the whole of last night.   7. They broke the news to her gently when she came back yesterday.   8. He shouted loudly over the telephone.   9. They were talking in low tones by the door when I came upon them.   10. The taxi stopped suddenly at the curb just now.   11. My uncle has been thinking it over carefully in his office for days.   12. He tiptoed quietly into the room last night and went to bed.   13. Did you water the plants regularly in my absence?   14. The train came into the station at one o'clock, and it left for Citiland an hour ago.

8–5 小練習

1. He will never realize his mistake.   2. She has always been kind to us.   3. Customers are generally hard to please.   4. That country has never been under foreign rule.   5. The turtles sometimes come to lay their eggs on the beach.   6. A tiger seldom kills a human being.   7. He is frequently absent from school.   8. Have you ever been to Italy?   9. You must always wash your hands before you eat.   10. Mosquitoes are usually found in swampy areas.   11. We seldom write letters these days.   12. They have never been to the zoo before.   13. The farmers usually harvest their crops in August.   14. Will she ever learn how to tie her shoelaces?   15. Do you generally plan your composition before you write it?   16. These birds are rarely seen outside the jungle.   17. We sometimes eat out in the evenings.   18. Why does Sally always come to school late?   19. Have you ever thought about going on a round-the-world trip?   20. I will always remember what happened at the seaside that day.

8-6 小練習

1. Only when he grows up will he understand the hardships of working for a living.   2. Rarely has she failed in her examinations.   3. Never in my life have I heard of such injustice.   4. Seldom have they been so late for the meeting.   5. So earnestly did the girls beg that their mother gave them what they wanted.   6. Never again will I do that without asking your advice first.   7. Hardly will you ever see old Mr. Jolly without a smile on his face.   8. So quietly did they do their work that the teacher suspected some mischief.   9. Soundly did the father spank his son.   10. He realized that only with supervision would the child perform his task.

應用練習

PART 1

1. gladly   2. skillfully   3. wisely   4. safely   5. politely   6. fiercely   7. freely   8. swiftly   9. seriously   10. untidily   11. dearly   12. painfully   13. joyfully   14. clumsily   15. actually   16. badly   17. nicely   18. loudly   19. forcefully   20. busily

PART 2

1. continually   2. efficiently   3. essentially   4. annoyingly   5. fixedly   6. really   7. possibly   8. wholly   9. duly   10. deep/deeply   11. quarterly   12. frantically   13. personally   14. surprisingly   15. uselessly   16. usually   17. minutely   18. relatively   19. humbly   20. rightly   21. high/highly   22. annually   23. mechanically   24. sheepishly   25. jokingly   26. wearily   27. healthily   28. suspiciously   29. hastily   30. energetically   31. boyishly   32. woodenly   33. satisfactorily   34. quickly   35. testily   36. volubly   37. loyally

PART 3

1. industriously   2. foggily   3. girlishly   4. gigantically   5. sunnily   6. systematically

7. attentively   8. gracefully   9. analytically   10. usefully   11. studiously   12. memorably

13. periodically   14. perfectly   15. perceptibly   16. kindly   17. luckily   18. favorably

19. peremptorily   20. noticeably   21. horribly   22. simply   23. inanely   24. excitedly   25. inaudibly

26. monstrously   27. nobly   28. legibly   29. daily   30. objectively

PART 4

1. We can harvest the crop even faster if we use that kind of machine.   2. This is quite the most impressive sculpture in the exhibition.   3. I was extremely sorry to hear of the tragic accident.   4. He has taken a few swimming lessons and he can swim fairly well now.   5. This is definitely the best film that I have ever seen.   6. The quality of this material is distinctly superior to that.   7. You are perfectly correct in your diagnosis.   8. It is only right that he should apologize to his cousin.   9. The crates of smuggled wine were partly concealed among the bushes.   10. This box is not big enough for us to put all these things in.   11. The picture that he recently drew is quite the best in the collection.   12. We were deeply sorry when we found out that we had accused him wrongly.   13. He didn't work quickly enough; that's why he was late.   14. They only believed half of what I said.   15. We were utterly dumbfounded when we saw him again.   16. The jug was practically empty when I first looked in it. Now it is almost full.   17. The village has changed enormously during the past few years. I can scarcely believe that it could change so fast.   18. "The fault is entirely yours." "No, it isn't. You are equally at fault."   19. This house isn't big enough to accommodate fifteen people. We need a much bigger house.

PART 5

1. It had been raining continuously here for the past week.   2. He lighted the firecracker carefully just now.   3. They shouted noisily from the window when they heard his call last night.   4. The wind was blowing strongly from the north.   5. She is seated in front, beside the man.   6. The workmen were chatting happily with each other all yesterday afternoon.   7. The children are hanging up their stockings in their rooms tonight.   8. The train came punctually into the station at nine o'clock.   9. The taxi driver braked noisily in front of the church.   10. They have been up Mount Fuji twice since last January.   11. The baby had been sleeping soundly in the next room for a few hours.   12. He had been ringing the doorbell insistently for about ten minutes.   13. The woman scolded the boy angrily in the garden last night.   14. The ship sailed for Sri Lanka at six o'clock yesterday morning.   15. The typhoon destroyed many houses on the island last month.

PART 6

1. I watered the plants on the front porch before having my dinner. 　2. The boy laughed heartily when he heard that last night. 　3. They had been discussing the matter thoroughly for half an hour before casting the vote. 　4. He got off the bus rather clumsily at the bus stop. 　5. Does she have to go to Sun Island with all of us immediately? 　6. Peter and Paul came here rather unexpectedly by bus yesterday evening. 　7. The car was very badly damaged in the accident yesterday. 　8. Aunt Polly put all the clothes neatly into the cupboard after folding them. 　9. A man grabbed me roughly on the dark street as I was passing by. 　10. The doorbell has been ringing on and off the whole day. 　11. The policeman was whistling softly as he cycled along the road early in the morning. 　12. She gave me a gift with a shy smile at my home during my birthday party. 　13. They willingly offered to give me a lift to my office in the mornings. 　14. We witnessed a serious accident at the intersection near the market last week.

PART 7

1. He pushed me roughly out of the way. 　2. John and Tom came home unexpectedly with some friends this morning. 　3. She put on her make-up carefully in front of the mirror after breakfast. 　4. They were watching television quietly when we came home last night. 　5. I did not go to the movies with my friends yesterday morning. 　6. The teacher scolded the naughty boy severely in class this morning. 　7. They saw a terribly frightening film at the Odeon last week. 　8. The students started giggling rather childishly when they heard the story. 　9. I packed all the clothes neatly into the suitcases after ironing them. 　10. Do we have to tell them the news when we meet them at Mary's house? 　11. The naughty boy fell rather heavily from the wall while watching the parade. 　12. Helen and her sisters had intended to go shopping along Trenton Street this morning. 　13. It hasn't been raining at all in this region for the past two months. 　14. Somebody has been trying to reach you urgently on the telephone the whole day. 　15. The girl accepted their good wishes and congratulations with a modest smile at her birthday party last night.

PART 8

1. He wanted to do that very much all his life. 　2. She is going to Sydney for two weeks on Monday. 　3. The students stayed quietly in class all morning. 　4. That old woman was born at four o'clock on Christmas morning in the year 1890. 　5. He has worked very hard in class throughout the week. 　6. She danced gracefully in the concert at the City Hall last week. 　7. Shall I meet you outside the movie theater at noon on Tuesday? 　8. He spoke to us rudely on our way to school this morning. 　9. The boy grinned sheepishly when he met us at the candy shop. 　10. He violently swerved to the pavement

when he rounded the corner.   11. I bought a pair of shoes at the annual sale in that shop last Saturday.
12. He arrived late at the office this morning.   13. The beggar told his tale pitifully as he sat on the sidewalk every day.   14. The boy angrily chased the goats out of the garden when he saw them eating the plants.   15. The runners ran around the field as fast as they could during the race.   16. He attentively listens to the teacher in the class every day.   17. The car accidentally ran over the dog while it was running across the road a few minutes ago.   18. I always do my homework in my room in the afternoon.   19. He rebuked the boy loudly when he saw him bullying another boy yesterday.   20. The robbery took place in the Galaxy Goldsmith shop at two o'clock in the afternoon.

PART 9

1. We went to the movies last night.   2. The jockeys led their horses to the racetrack when the order was given.   3. The Russian troupe performed excellently at the Cultural Hall last month.   4. The dog barked loudly when I opened the gate last night.   5. We have tea under the tree in the garden every day.
6. We went home immediately after work.   7. The sheep protested noisily when the shearers started working on them.   8. Mike has acted in a strange manner since the day that he saw the accident.   9. He scolded the boy angrily when he caught him stealing the fruit yesterday.   10. Peter shouted "Fire! Fire!" loudly when he saw smoke coming out of the house last night.   11. The accident occurred outside the hospital in the afternoon.   12. The "lion dance" was performed outside the town hall last Sunday.
13. The children were playing joyfully in the shallow river when it started to rain.   14. The man talked eloquently at the dinner.   15. A stranger came up to us suddenly as we were walking home last night.
16. The acrobat jumped nimbly over the wall when he heard a cry for help.   17. The boy carefully helped the blind man across the street just now.   18. The twins were born at the District Hospital at four o'clock on New Year's Day in 1960.   19. The guard crept cautiously around the office building when he heard some sounds.   20. The athlete threw the javelin as far as he could at the sports meet last week.

PART 10

1. He has never met with an accident in his car before.   2. These boys are always punished for their mistakes.   3. The train is often delayed these days.   4. He sometimes sets mousetraps in his house.
5. Her relatives usually stay until the visiting hours are over.   6. Has he ever been to Windy Hill?   7. Parents are always invited to the prize-giving ceremony each year.   8. Frogs usually come out after it rains.   9. The shops are generally full of customers on Saturdays.   10. He rarely loses his temper with his children.   11. She sometimes sleeps on the top bunk.   12. "Have you ever seen a gold coin?" "No, I have never seen one."   13. This kind of bird is rarely seen near where people live.   14. Tourists usually

stay in that hotel.　15. He sometimes forgets to lock his room before he goes out.　16. That boy always forgets when the meetings are supposed to begin.　17. The boys have occasionally been punished for ill-treating the neighbors' cats.　18. Do they frequently swim in that stream near the edge of the jungle?　19. His mother has often told him not to play in the street.　20. This is the first time anyone has ever treated me this way.

PART 11

1. You rarely see such good performances in circuses of this type.　2. I nearly always manage to reach home in time to watch my favorite television program.　3. She always does everything neatly; she is never untidy, and she seldom makes a place dirty.　4. They usually pass her house on their way to school.　5. Do you know why Robert always comes to school late?　6. They had already been waiting for over an hour when we arrived.　7. I have seldom enjoyed myself so much at a party as I've done at this one.　8. These girls are never punctual when there is a meeting.　9. The absent-minded old man frequently sends his letters to the wrong addresses.　10. Her mother has repeatedly told her never to go home later than ten; but she seldom obeys.　11. He rarely visits his Aunt Sally, but he frequently drops in at Aunt Mary's house.　12. "Has your pressure cooker ever given you any trouble?" "No, it hasn't. It always runs smoothly."　13. I do not remember ever having met him.　14. He has occasionally been disobedient.　15. We seldom see him these days.　16. He has been here twice but he hardly remembers anything.　17. None of us had ever been there before.　18. You should always do as your elders tell you.　19. You must never get off a bus when it is moving.　20. I would never have known what to do if you had not always guided me.

PART 12

1. That scientist usually goes to bed at four in the morning.　2. I have often been told to report to him. 3. She has never been there before.　4. He is scarcely ever at home.　5. He occasionally has lunch in the office.　6. Mr. Lewis rarely smiles at us these days.　7. You will never see such a sight again. 8. The old woman visits her doctor regularly.　9. He has never done such a thing before.　10. He was seldom absent from work in the mine.　11. This is the most memorable day in my life; I will always remember it.　12. The President is often accompanied by his bodyguards.　13. "Do you always read in bed?" "Yes, I always do."　14. I generally get up with the dawn.　15. The doctor always advised the old woman to take her medicine regularly.　16. I have repeatedly told him not to play in the rain but he nearly always does.　17. Previously he often had nightmares and now he has them occasionally.　18. Don't ever do that again; you cannot always get away with it.　19. I sometimes walk in the woods by

myself and after these walks I generally feel happier.

Chapter 9　解答

9–1 小練習

1. drowsier　　2. younger　　3. wealthiest　　4. more surprised　　5. paler; thinner; heaviest; lighter

6. tastier　　7. more successful　　8. least　　9. more; most　　10. hardest; most delicious

11. more comfortable; more expensive　　12. worse　　13. best; most bitter

14. easiest; more confident; fullest

9–2 小練習

1. farther/further; farthest/furthest　　2. more easily; most easily　　3. less; least

4. more tastefully; most tastefully　　5. more softly; most softly　　6. more tearfully; most tearfully

7. more excitedly; most excitedly　　8. more gleefully; most gleefully　　9. more visibly; most visibly

10. more profusely; most profusely　　11. more neatly; most neatly　　12. more attentively; most attentively

13. more dangerously; most dangerously　　14. more disgracefully; most disgracefully

15. more strangely; most strangely　　16. earlier; earliest　　17. later/latter; latest/last

18. more cleverly; most cleverly　　19. more dirtily; most dirtily　　20. straighter; straightest

21. more bitterly; most bitterly　　22. more purposely; most purposely　　23. more simply; most simply

24. more permanently; most permanently　　25. more happily; most happily　　26. more; most

27. more highly; most highly　　28. faster; fastest　　29. worse; worst　　30. better; best

31. more loudly; most loudly　　32. nearer; nearest

9–3 小練習

1. better; harder　　2. hungry; much　　3. faster　　4. most popular　　5. more careful; less; better

6. more; happier　　7. earlier; earliest　　8. most important; most important

9. least developed; widest　　10. most; busiest　　11. worse; worse; better　　12. angrier; better

9–4 小練習

1. latter; older　　2. older　　3. farther　　4. fewer; less　　5. better; last　　6. further　　7. farthest

8. oldest; oldest/eldest　　9. last; further　　10. latter; faster　　11. oldest/eldest; better; youngest

12. latest; more efficiently　　13. nearest; further　　14. latest; fewer　　15. fewest; last

16. eldest; older; youngest　　17. last; further　　18. oldest/eldest; cleverest　　19. farthest; least

20. elder; older; eldest/oldest　　21. further　　22. elder; older　　23. elder; older; younger

24. youngest; oldest; older　　25. eldest/oldest; older; older　　26. later; farther; elder

應用練習

PART 1

1. more lovingly; most lovingly   2. slyer; slyest   3. more plainly; most plainly

4. more fearful; most fearful   5. more misleading; most misleading   6. more attractively; most attractively   7. sturdier; sturdiest   8. more craftily; most craftily

9. punier; puniest   10. more strongly; most strongly   11. fewer; fewest

12. more merrily; most merrily   13. eviler; evilest   14. more amazing; most amazing

15. more splendidly; most splendidly   16. feebler; feeblest   17. harsher; harshest

18. more apt; most apt   19. cheekier; cheekiest   20. more frightfully; most frightfully

21. more renowned; most renowned   22. sterner; sternest   23. more speedily; most speedily

24. more marvelous; most marvelous   25. more thankfully; most thankfully

26. more dependable; most dependable   27. more courageous; most courageous   28. gladder; gladdest

PART 2

1. simpler; simplest   2. finer; finest   3. more sadly; most sadly   4. grayer; grayest

5. more barren; most barren   6. more commonly; most commonly

7. more pleasantly; most pleasantly   8. quieter; quietest   9. more handsome; most handsome

10. more polite; most polite   11. more; most   12. older/elder; oldest/eldest   13. abler; ablest

14. more rapidly; most rapidly   15. more common; most common   16. more miserable; most miserable

17. more pleasant; most pleasant   18. moodier; moodiest   19. narrower; narrowest

20. more extravagant; most extravagant   21. more swiftly; most swiftly   22. faster; fastest

23. sooner; soonest   24. more immense; most immense   25. thinner; thinnest   26. bigger; biggest

27. more cheerfully; most cheerfully   28. more superior; most superior

PART 3

1. shorter   2. more; more often   3. most experienced   4. best   5. more heavily

6. large; smallest   7. most accurate; faster   8. easier; most difficult   9. lighter; less; heaviest

10. fatter; healthy   11. worst; better; little   12. oldest; prettiest   13. worse; worse   14. farther; worst

15. More; more

PART 4

1. kindest   2. intelligent   3. better; best   4. clearer   5. more carefully; better   6. greener

7. early; earlier; early   8. cheaply; more cheaply; most cheaply   9. well; worse; worse

10. less; less   11. most advanced; highest   12. cleverer

PART 5

1. highest   2. more expensive   3. dangerous   4. faster; fastest   5. best   6. richest   7. hotter

8. cutest   9. stronger   10. beautiful; more beautiful   11. highest; taller   12. better; most beautifully

13. thickest; thicker   14. distinctly; farther; less   15. youngest; cheekiest   16. later

17. oldest/eldest; greater   18. deeper; more difficult   19. fast; nearer; nearer   20. more sweetly; prettier

PART 6

1. most   2. more; less   3. further   4. worst   5. longer; more dangerous   6. highest

7. most expensive; most valuable   8. worse   9. better   10. stronger; healthier   11. easier

12. sharper   13. darker; more cheerful   14. early   15. thicker   16. more careful   17. more brightly

18. older; wiser; more   19. weaker; worse; worse   20. more; fewer

PART 7

1. better   2. big; smaller   3. hotter; hot   4. more; hungrier   5. more; fewer   6. more; less

7. more sweetly; best   8. more careful; safer   9. stronger; rough; gentler

10. more heavily; more soundly   11. older/elder; less; younger

12. best; cheapest; least dangerous; most economical   13. most; fewest; many; more

PART 8

1. cheaper; faster   2. younger; more intelligent; more hardworking   3. heavy; clumsier

4. most beautiful; speediest   5. better; cheaper   6. more; quickly   7. worse; more heavily

8. better; harder   9. most interesting; interesting   10. coldest; more; more soundly   11. best; better

12. earlier; later; fresh   13. elder; prettier; younger; younger; more intelligent

14. least; slower; most; later

PART 9

1. further; last   2. least   3. farther; more tired; more   4. more successful; fewer; last

5. latter; older   6. farther; more thickly; oldest; last   7. latest; more efficiently

8. worst; harder; worse   9. less; farther; more likely   10. farthest; most talkative   11. latest; farthest

12. least; farthest   13. latter; more afraid; more hesitant   14. most unfortunate; later; further

PART 10

1. fewer; less   2. studious; more   3. youngest; most intelligent; highest   4. better; more expressive

5. more; angrier   6. cleverest; most beautiful; worst   7. obstinate; younger; more friendly

8. simplest; most effective   9. well; more   10. more; less; more desperate; nearer

11. longer; more; more secure   12. more pleased   13. longest; largest

基礎文法寶典 ❷
Essential English Usage & Grammar

14. most frightful; more unfriendly; more terrifying   15. lightest; most soothing

16. liveliest; most colorful; most spectacular   17. more worried; better; worse

18. impressive; more interesting; more frequently   19. deepest; strongest; most dangerous

PART 11

1. more beautiful   2. faster; sooner   3. most interesting   4. worse   5. stronger; stronger

6. higher; higher   7. stubborn; bad-tempered   8. worst; worst   9. less; more tired

10. most impolite   11. most well-mannered; most helpful; most hardworking   12. more; less

13. more; angrier   14. most attractive   15. lowest   16. higher; higher; more resourceful

PART 12

1. of   2. than   3. to   4. a   5. less expensive/cheaper   6. than   7. worse   8. more

9. better   10. better   11. to; as   12. as; as   13. more   14. eldest; than; youngest; younger; older

English Grammar Juncture

英文文法階梯

康雅蘭 嚴雅貞　編著

專為想要重新學好文法的讀者
所編寫的初級文法教材

- 一網打盡高中職各家版本英文課程所要求的文法基礎，為往後的英語學習打下良好基礎。

- 盡量以句型呈現文法，避免冗長解說，配上簡單易懂的例句，讓學習者在最短時間內掌握重點，建立整體架構。

- 除高中職學生外，也適合讓想要重新自修英文文法的讀者溫故知新之用。

Practical English Grammar

實用英文文法（完整版）

馬洵 劉紅英 郭立穎　編著
龔慧懿　編審

專為大專學生及在職人士學習英語所編寫的實用文法教材

- 涵蓋英文文法、詞彙分類、句子結構及常用句型。
- 凸顯實用英文文法，定義力求簡明扼要，以圖表條列方式歸納文法重點，概念一目了然。
- 搭配大量例句，情境兼具普遍與專業性，中文翻譯對照，方便自我進修學習。

實用英文文法實戰題本

馬洵 劉紅英　編著

- 完全依據《實用英文文法》出題，實際活用文法概念。
- 試題數量充足，題型涵蓋廣泛，內容符合不同程度讀者需求。
- 除每章的練習題外，另有九回綜合複習試題，加強學習效果。
- 搭配詳盡試題解析本，即時釐清文法學習要點。